FRAGMENTS OF THE PAST

JODY KAYE

Splinter of Hope
Shred of Decency
Sliver of Truth
Holding Onto Hope
Home Wrecker
Deep Gap
Bleeding Heart
Shattered Soul

Fragments of the Past

Sometimes it's'a relief
pretending be someone I'm not
...Someone normal.

For Sarah

Chapter One

Rae Lee

"Your name is Raleigh?" he asks with a raised brow. The left-hand corner of his mouth tips up in a lopsided grin as he lifts his beer bottle closer to his suckable lower lip.

I ambush him with an imperceptible jerk of my head and smile.

He's gotten it wrong. But over the din of the crowd, I can't blame him for mishearing.

Living this close to the North Carolina state capital, he also seems to like the novelty of Raleigh. So why not? After all, I came to Sweet Caroline's tonight to escape the trappings of being Rae Lee Chatham.

Fans mob the concert hall. With this many people trying to make themselves heard before the opening act even takes the stage, I won't have to listen to anyone or anything I don't want to tonight. I like the easy attention of the man whose blatant interest in me is uncomplicated, and I'd like nothing more than to talk to him uninterrupted. Maybe later, after the curtain call, we'll use our mouths to communicate in a different way.

Leaning his hip against the bar, his gaze hovers at the neckline of my unbuttoned white shirt. The lace of a periwinkle blue bralette plays peekaboo, enhancing my cleavage. The honky tonk's dim lighting makes his brownish-black irises dark and his wide pupils darker. He has thick lashes, the kind falsie-wearing girls are jealous of. If it weren't for the lighter shade of brown hair, he'd be otherworldly. Although it's a peculiar talent, I'm good at reading people, and nothing about him screams danger.

He's just a guy looking for a good time. And by the looks of this man, he can give me a very good time.

Isn't that why I'm here? To forget my troubles and enjoy life?

With a self-assured grin, he continues his perusal of my body. From the pressed shirt to my skirt to the embroidered booties with a slight heel, I've dressed for the occasion. I'm equally unashamed letting my attention roam and feeding his ego.

When he's done drinking me in, he holds his hand out to introduce himself.

"Anson. Can I get you a refill?" He swallows the last swig of his beer and offers to buy my next one.

"Sure." I wiggle the empty by the neck. Anson takes it, turning toward the bartender to get us two more.

I close my eyes and bite my lower lip, wishing it was because I was reveling in the way his back muscles ripple underneath the fabric of his polo shirt.

Fudge… I mouth, though anyone in the vicinity would think I used the other F word.

If I were anyplace else, needing anything else, I would ask his last name. But last names don't matter in the morning. Not when you aren't planning to see the other person again.

I ignore the voice inside of me that's trying to tell me that if Anson heard me correctly, he'd be the one to put the brakes on. The likelihood that there are a lot of Ansons running around Brighton as there are Rae Lee's is virtually nil. Putting everyone else's needs before mine is exhausting, and the reward for doing the right thing is shittastic.

If he is the Anson who contacted me, then the itch I came here to scratch will continue to haunt me. If he isn't, and I fess up my name is not Raleigh, the ensuing pointless and awkward apologies will turn me into a blithering idiot. Either way, whatever drew us together gets dusted. Overall, I'm also not particularly interested in having any conversations with Anson Ames tonight. Whatever he has to say can wait until tomorrow.

I flick my conscience off my shoulder.

Grasping two cold tan bottles, Anson returns his attention to me. At the same moment, I pretend I don't see the crestfallen older man with chiseled Norse features sitting in a round booth that was removed when Sweet Caroline's was remodeled. I need that mirage to disappear so I can focus on the real, live man in front of me.

Anson watches me down half the beer in two long gulps. "Thirsty?"

"You could say that." A single shoulder of mine bounces.

"As long as you're not drinking to forget."

I step into his space. My toes tip up in my short boots and I clutch the front of his shirt above his navel for balance. "What if I were?" I whisper in his ear.

Anson turns his face toward mine. "Then that would make two of us." He tips his beer towards me in a mock-salute and brings it to his lips, taking long, hard pulls.

The curtain rises and the drummer for the band responsible for warming up the crowd taps out the first few beats.

"Let's dance." Anson grabs my hand, dragging me towards the stage.

We're two grown adults, and his desire for Raleigh makes it easy to leave any misgivings behind.

Anson pats his pockets, searching for his keys. I stand to the side, trying to keep out of his way. He slips one hand on my hip to stop me from moving too far away and uses the other to unlock the front door to his condo. It gives me a moment to study his laugh lines, the deep creases below his temples, and the fine premature gray strands glinting in the streetlight. Dancing in the dark at Sweet Caroline's, he had a youthful appearance. Although people who have stressful careers tend to age faster. Perhaps he's as young as I pegged him to be and it's whatever Anson has witnessed that weighs on him.

Lord knows that's how it goes for me.

I run my fingers over the scruff of his cheek. The lock clicks in time with him giving me his full attention. His lips press to my knuckles. My palm moves to the back of his neck and we're kissing again, rolling inside of his foyer, connected as close as we'd been on the dance floor.

We'd only stopped dancing to refill our drinks, and partway through the concert for me to take a fun selfie of the two of us. The headliner was poised behind us, catching his breath and chatting up the crowd. I sent the snapshot to my friend, Layla—something Anson didn't seem to mind.

I would have sent it no matter what. A woman

can't be too careful.

Anson has me pinned against the wall. The door shuts and we're bathed in blue shadows. My palms clutch his shoulders as he plunders my mouth. I hear his keys clink into a bowl. The thick bulge in his pants presses against me as he kicks his shoes to the side.

In my peripheral vision, I see a stacking rack filled with several pairs of loafers. I award him imaginary bonus points for being conscientious. You never know what the soles track in from outside, contaminating your safe surroundings. There's also nothing worse than going home with an incredibly sexy, well-dressed man other than finding out he's a slob. The sloven are more interested in getting their jollies rather than getting anyone else off.

He dips his lips to my neck, nipping and biting. "Are you sure about this?"

I moan my assent. That should be all it takes. Yet, all of a sudden, were nose to nose. Anson wants me to articulate when all I want is for our bodies to communicate.

I take his imaginary bonus points back.

Okay, half of them. Only the best of the best men don't take consent for granted. I appreciate the respect he's showing.

"Yes. I'm sure." I suck his lower lip between mine.

Anson patiently waits for me to remove my boots. He smirks at the inches it takes off my height when I'm in stocking feet. Similar to the way he pulled me to the dance floor, he moves us up a short flight of stairs.

To the right, I can make out the silvery kitchen appliances because of the range hood nightlight. To the left, is another flight of stairs. In front of us, a lamp illuminates the corner of the living room. In the daylight, the walls must be a light yellow as the light cast makes the tone beige.

He sits down on a deep navy sofa. The plush kind with attached pillows on the back. The style is so humorously basic that every furniture store stocks a variation, and depending on where you shop determines how much you pay. I fall onto his lap, comfortable with Anson and his no-frills bachelor pad.

He has the buttons of my shirt undone in a heartbeat and his thumb grazes my stomach below the lace of my periwinkle bralette. His hand rides higher, cupping and squeezing my tit over my bra. Breaking another kiss, I'm enamored by the reverence of each layer being peeled away and how slowly he's taking it for how fast we are moving.

I lift the hem of his shirt. It goes over his head, revealing his broad chest to my touch. I stroke a hand over the taut muscles. It's apt that he wears a St. Rita medal on a chain. She's the patron saint of impossible causes. Between Anson's soft, flat nipples is a triangle patch with a trace of hair. Not too faint and not too thick.

I shift my legs off of Anson's lap and fall between

his knees. Twisting so that I'm kneeling on the floor, I reach and unbuckle his belt. Anson lifts his hips. I tug and he shimmies. His boxers slide down his legs along with his pants. His erection springs free. The bulging veins of his cock look harsh in this light, painful. My only thoughts are about how to ease the hurt.

He takes a sharp breath, hissing at my teasing tongue flicking the bead of pre-cum off the mushroom head. His teeth clench when my nails tickle the underside of his sac. Having wanted to watch him come undone since the first slide of heat against my body while we danced, I wrap my hand around his engorged length. He covers it with his own, breathing heavily, and showing me what he likes.

I glance up at him from under my lashes. Pain and pleasure are written all over his face. He enjoys each circular jerk of our wrists. Unabashed men willing to help me masturbate them make every erogenous zone in my body tingle. I have a feeling, given more than one encounter, having him between my thighs could bring me to tears. The hurt-so-good kind that leaves your knees wobbly and you begging for him to never stop.

The roughened thumb of the hand he held his cock with caresses my cheek. "Open."

He pinches the skin at my jawbone, and I obey. My already damp panties are no match for the mouth-watering glory before me, anyway. I want this. My lips part and I flick my tongue out, licking his cock from root to tip. I play demure so that he'll wonder if I think he's big, which I do. But my experience with men is that they enjoy believing they are more than a mouthful. And yes, Anson is, so it's not as much of an act as I've put on before.

"Take as much as you can," he encourages, putting light pressure on the back of my skull as I bob up and down. "Take it all."

I hum, stroking and squeezing. His hips thrust up of their own volition.

"Fuck, you're good at that." He threads his fingers through my blonde hair. Gathering it in his fist, he pops me off, grunting, "Get up here before I come down your throat."

I rise, placing a knee on either side of his lap to straddle him. Anson takes advantage of my flouncing skirt. He tucks his hand below the hem and moves my soaked panties to the side.

I grab his face, thrusting my tongue into his mouth the second he spears me with two fingers. I let out a keening moan as his palm skids over my sensitive flesh. The man knows just how to touch me. I lean back, lifting my skirt over my thighs for a better view of Anson finger fucking me.

"You like that? My fingers in your pussy?"

"God, yes!" I pant, the tightness building at the apex of my sex. I reach to pump him, not knowing how much longer I have until the wave of bliss breaks over me and I become incoherent.

"I don't think you're ready to sit on my cock just yet, baby. Prove to my fingers what my dick has to look forward to."

At this filthy request, I explode. Anson coaxes the last violent shudders from me. He drags his pants from where they landed on the couch cushion. The only fumbling he's done the entire night is removing his wallet from the back pocket. Inside a foil packet glints. It doesn't stay sealed long.

Chapter Two

Rae Lee

"Are you sticking around?" Anson's body covers mine. His nose travels the length of my clavicle, ending with a soft kiss he places on my shoulder.

The medal on the necklace he's wearing is smooth. I play with the chain, swirling my fingers in the fine hair at the base of his skull.

We never left the couch. I'm not even fully naked. My rumpled skirt is flipped over my belly and my bralette is stretched out of place. My neck and left breast have beard burn, though there's something soothing about the warm, firm skin of his bare pec that flattens my tit to my chest.

Pinned, I shrug in a "why not" manner.

Anson sits, pulls his boxers over his hips, and pads to the bathroom. After cleaning up, he stretches out beside me on his side, taking the spot on the sofa closest to the cushy pillow back. There's not a lot of room for two people on the couch. He makes sure I'm comfortable on my back. Then he flips off the side lamp and drapes an arm over me.

Minutes later, Anson's chest rises and falls in a soothing rhythm. However, I'm wide awake, trying not to fidget.

I don't dislike being held afterward, but the awkwardness of staying until the sun rises and bumbling goodbyes aren't enjoyable for anyone. I slide out from his embrace and grab my shirt from the floor.

"Where are you going?" His voice is sleep laden.

"Bathroom." I slip my shirt on while tip-toeing towards the stairs, where I saw him go before. "Go back to sleep."

Coming up short at the threshold to the kitchen, there is a blonde woman hovering inside the room. Her expression isn't readable. At first glance, I thought she was content. But the jealousy emanating from her is undeniable.

"Oh, shit," I gasp. Recognizing who she is, my fingers stretch out in front of me. "Angeline?" I whisper, but she's gone.

I step into the kitchen, momentarily glad that Anson is a conscientious leave-a-light-on kind of guy. When I see the gold crest of his badge sitting on a laptop as quiet as a mouse, I decide to disappear, too.

I prefer quality friendships over quantity. The

people who know the real Rae Lee are few. If anyone asked Layla, who I sent the selfie of Anson and me at Sweet Caroline's to, she'd be the last to say I was reckless, especially not with my heart. Yet, she'd be the first to say my infrequent hookups with men—whom I don't necessarily want to discuss world events over breakfast with— were cavalier. Hence, her insistence on an in-focus headshot to ensure my safety.

Though if she had to give the photo over to the police or pick the guy out in a line up, there's probably not much hope for me, is there?

Failing to correct Anson when he misheard my name was foolhardy. In retrospect, I had a lot of audacity. Exactly whose eyes was I thinking I could pull the wool over on?

Besides mine.

I can't blame the booze. And my resentment about not feeling normal won't gain me sympathy when my hasty, but panty-melting amazing, fucking mistake figures out who I am.

Detective Anson Ames of the Brighton Police Department contacted me last week. I've assisted in a dozen cases in Eastern North Carolina but stopped years ago. Whether their duty is to remain impartial as they collect evidence or not, I don't particularly like the suspicion I'm met with by the police. Not when they are the ones who seek me out, anyway. Just because skepticism is their job doesn't mean I have to subject myself to it. Guarding not only my health, but my mental health in situations where grizzlier crimes have taken place takes precedence.

My abilities are no good to anyone if I'm run down. Opening up to the spirit world has lasting effects. It left me with medical diagnoses I wouldn't wish upon my enemies—if I surrounded myself with adequate people outside of my small circle of friends to have any.

I'd broken my rule, refusing to get involved for two reasons. First, I'd consulted on a case with Angeline McCuller. At the time, she was with a neighboring police department and the viable leads were dwindling. She'd been scrupulous but kind. Quite honestly, everything about her mannerisms screamed of the golden rule.

It's also why I somewhat forgive—and also don't fully comprehend—her reaction to me earlier this morning. I suppose it doesn't take a genius to figure out that Angeline is protective of Anson. He identified her on the phone as a reliable friend. I got the sense he was devoted to her, or at least to honoring her memory.

Second, Detective Ames stated the victim's family had pushed for a medium to get involved. I'm not interested in handing out a business card proffering my services and trying to pump up business. However, I'd question my own humanity if I didn't have sympathy for people who believed you were their last-ditch effort to gain closure.

How can you say no to another human who has had the courage to hold onto hope in the bleakest of circumstances?

I walk the quiet downtown streets with my thumb poised over the emergency call button on my cell. My apartment isn't far from Anson's place. He lives in one of those shiny new live/work/play complexes that are all the rage. I live in the only loft unit on the second floor of an old mansion. It's located in the historic district on the opposite side of the street and a few blocks down from the concert hall.

At home, the door bounces off of an unopened box of kitty litter. I shower, change, fall into bed and sleep until my alarm goes off past noon. I pour milk over a bowl of strawberry flavored shredded wheat, then sit alone at the small table, letting the biscuits go soggy. I throw them down the sink and flick on the loud garbage disposal, which eats my breakfast for me.

Stumbling back to the facilities, I accidentally—or intentionally—kick the bag of cat food that needs to go to the animal shelter. I stand under the shower stream. Hot tears of frustration trail down my cheeks. I wipe the snot from my nose. The water from my body. Finally, I slip into a professional black pencil skirt and scoop the tan and cream retro-style kitten heels with a buckle over the bridge of my foot from the pile of shoes by the door.

I don't have a shoe rack. Sue me.

A blouse similar to what I wore last night finishes the ensemble. This time it's sheer, buttoned to my throat with what your mother would call "appropriate" undergarments instead of ones that tempt a glance.

My phone with the constant low battery has enough juice to alert me that the rideshare I ordered is waiting outside. So that it doesn't influence what I see, I'm kept in the dark about the places I visit. I tap the screen and show the driver a pdf I haven't opened before listing the address I'm headed to.

The ride share driver stops a good ten miles away on a residential street. I recognize the other vehicle in front of the house as the same one I slid by while entering the condo past midnight. Detective Ames waits in the driver's seat.

I don't have much of a reputation, but as we both exit the cars we've traveled in, I can admit it's tarnished.

Detective Ames clenches his jaw. If he bared his teeth, I'd expect him to snap and bite. "It's you."

I should hold out my hand, but I tuck a strand of hair behind my ear instead. "Yeah, me." I sigh, ready to apologize. "I know this is unorthodox, but —"

"Which part exactly? Lying to me, or the charade you're about to pull on the Turners?" His hands find his waist, pushing his sport coat behind his hips and revealing his holster. The motion pulls the fabric of his thin-striped plaid button-down taut.

I swallow both out of regret and lingering desire,

remembering the breadth of his chest. Sun glints off his badge, which is affixed to his jeans. But the time to revel in his rugged good looks or the take-charge attitude that had increased my attraction to him once we were alone has passed. Anson Ames spits venom at me.

"You know what? It doesn't matter. Let's get this shit show over with. Do you want me to introduce you as Miss Chatham?"

"Rae Lee is fine."

"Yeah, whatever," he mutters, giving me his back. Detective Ames doesn't wait, storming up the walkway towards the front door.

I follow with my eyes downcast, focusing on the worn spots on the underside of his loafers. As we approach the house, I release the barriers I'd held tightly to the previous evening. Opening my mind, I perceive everything Detective Ames brought me to this house in search of.

He rings the bell. An older couple answers the door. Detective Ames makes the briefest of introductions. I see matched skepticism to the detective's etched on the Turners' faces... And the underlying, unyielding hope that someday someone will provide them with answers.

I also see what they can't.

The four of us enter the living room, but we aren't alone. Unbeknownst to Susan Turner, a twelve-year-old girl sidles up next to her. The child clasps her hand around her mother's forearm. Mrs. Turner frowns. Her opposite hand brushes the sensation away, and the girl takes a step back.

Sadness washes over me.

The fearful child is why I'm here. Sometimes, she cries when Mrs. Turner dismisses the attempts she makes to gain her mother's attention.

I see something gray and sparkly and a brilliant white openness.

"Your daughter was named after a gem," I blurt.

"Pearl."

"That's a beautiful name."

"Thank you. It was my first husband's mother's. Am I allowed to tell you that?"

"Maybe stick to yes or no," Detective Ames suggests kindly to Mrs. Turner. I receive a glare.

"That would be best," I agree, pretending I'm oblivious to his ire.

"You and Pearl don't use the same last name?"

"No." Mrs. Turner looks at her husband, Harvey, desperate to elaborate.

"Do you have any other children?" Mr. Turner stands closer to me. I move, focusing the questions on Mrs. Turner.

"No."

"Not for lack of trying." Mr. Turner flashes me a grin that feels like I've gotten hit by a sledgehammer. My belly sinks and rolls. I'm nauseous as he hugs his wife from the side.

"Oh, good." I bob my head, looking around the room.

"I had several… losses. After losing Pearl. Maybe I was just supposed to be her mom." Mrs. Turner rests her head on Harvey's shoulder. Her eyes brim with tears.

I'd express sympathy, but I don't have the least bit of remorse, and Pearl isn't sorry either.

I see the little girl age down. She's seven or eight now, angrily sending her fist through Mrs. Turner's lower gut. She tries to shove Mr. Turner out of the way. She fights him like an animal, clawing and punching.

Something skitters up my thigh, and my heart begins to race. Oh, this is not good.

"I gather you're not Pearl's father?"

"Her dad was my business partner. He died before Pearl vanished."

Early death. Natural causes. Well, I mean, heart attacks aren't classified as foul play, are they?

The hatred Pearl has for Harvey Turner surges over me and I wince.

"Would you... Could you leave for a few minutes, Mr. Turner? I'm sorry." I apologize to Mrs. Turner out of politeness. "I'm—" I shake my head and push my palms to my cheeks. "I'm feeling a little distracted. As if the puzzle pieces I have need to be rotated around." My fingers pinch into the ASL sign for more and twist. "They're stuck." And where I don't know the exact reason I'm here other than the unmistakable—Pearl isn't among the living. "Your husband can come back later." Hopefully, when I'm gone.

Mr. Turner exits the room. I double over with nausea, grabbing my knees. The last thing I had in my stomach was beer. I probably should have choked down the cereal.

"Would you like to sit?" Detective Ames places a palm on my back and holds me steady by the arm. "We'd like to finish this today." There's no inflection in his voice, but the threat is obvious. *Don't play me for a fool again.*

"I'll be okay." I breathe deeply, trying to center myself. I doubt breaking the news will come as a shock to Mrs. Turner. "Your daughter passed away when she was young."

Mrs. Turner inhales sharply. Her lips pinch and her chin trembles. The news isn't anything she hasn't already accepted. Her grief washes over me. She removes a tissue from her pocket and wipes her nose and the tears trailing down her cheeks. "Yes," she finally responds after composing herself.

"You never got her body back." The statement feels obvious.

Pearl's mother shakes her head back and forth, dabbing at her red eyes.

"Can you tell us anything about the night Pearl disappeared?" Detective Ames cuts to the chase.

"She says she left on a dare," I wince, reaching up to clutch the side of my head. My left temple feels hot and prickly, like something is pouring down my face. My vision blurs on that side. I think it's blood.

Chapter Three

Anson

We haven't been on this ridiculous ghost walk at the Turner residence for long and already I'd prefer if Rae Lee Chatham used her mouth to do something else.

Like shut the hell up.

The last thing I want is for a "psychic medium" to get this mother's hopes up. Mrs. Turner has been through enough. She doesn't deserve to be lied to about her daughter's disappearance.

Why did you agree to this? I think, not for the first time.

I'd wanted to remain open-minded about Mrs. Turner's dubious request. After all, Angeline gave me the impression she was happy with Miss Chatham's unique services. They'd broken a case for her. At the very least, I wasn't searching for another needle in a haystack trying to find a reputable seer who "spoke with the dead."

Speaking with the dead. Yeah, right.

My tolerance for paranormal speculation has dipped to an all-time low. Given that *Rae Lee* used that sweet mouth to lead me on, I don't believe a word out of it.

I hide a scoff for Mrs. Turner's benefit. Victims' families are already upset. They relive their trauma the second their eyes open in the morning. But days like today slice open old wounds. My own relationship with grief grounds me. I have no intention of making it any harder for the Turners than it already is.

Pearl Tatton disappeared from her family's Brighton home fifteen years ago. The middle schooler was in the seventh grade, a month shy of her thirteenth birthday. The majority of the pictures her mother provided in the wake of her disappearance were of Pearl with her father, who had passed away eighteen months prior.

Mr. Tatton suffered from congenital heart failure throughout most of Pearl's late childhood. According to Mrs. Tatton's statements, encouraged by his cardiologist's, Mr. Tatton tried his hardest to be there for his child. He had even coached her softball team during the final season he was alive. The newer pictures of Pearl wearing eyeshadow and lip gloss were ones her best friend's parents shared with the original investigators.

That isn't to say Pearl was engaging in any

activities that were unusual for a person of her age. My parents were blessed with Irish triplets. By the time I was Pearl's age, my older and younger sisters had filled the bathroom with razors, fruit scented shampoos, and all sorts of lotions and potions that made the head of a prepubescent boy spin. What on earth did they need all that perfume shit for? And then there were the bras hanging from the rod every time I went to shower. So many freakin' bras. Meanwhile, I swiped the soap over my nuts and hoped my mom didn't realize I put back on the same pair of soiled underwear.

Twelve is different for boys. A report stating Pearl wasn't concerned about her clothes and outward appearance, or that her friends thought she carried the scent of a dirty laundry basket, would send up red flags.

By all accounts, Pearl was polite and well-mannered. Her teachers described her as a joy to have in class. Inquisitive. Never late with her assignments. Always willing to go the extra mile to make an outcast feel included.

Having already lost her spouse, I wonder if Pearl's mother simply wished to stop time and that's why she hadn't noticed the absence of a single school portrait. Her child had begun to bloom, transforming beyond the years spent as a family. The psychology of trauma is interesting. The way it manifests is often so inexplicably simplistic that it gets overlooked or, on the contrary, becomes the focal point of dead-end leads.

Mrs. Tatton was also preoccupied, having become responsible for her late-husband's percentage of Tatton & Turner. On the night in question, she and Mr. Turner had been out for the evening—providing the now Mrs. Turner's new husband a solid alibi. The case file includes the receipts for their dinner, as well as sworn affidavits from the waitstaff at the restaurant they'd eaten at. Mr. and Mrs. Turner married eight months after Pearl vanished.

There was no indication anyone broke into the home. Initial reports suggested Pearl ran away, though there was blood evidence collected from the hallway bathroom matching Pearl's. Like the parents of most runaways, Mrs. Turner refused to leave the house her daughter grew up in on the off chance that Pearl ever came back.

Detectives questioned the employees at Tatton & Turner, their family, and friends. No one seemed to have a beef with the Turners. Everyone seemed to share Pearl's mother's devastation, having lost not only her husband, but her only child.

Six months later, an eighth-grader went missing in a nearby town. Then, after another two weeks, a sixth-grade girl in Raleigh. The other divisions in conjunction with Brighton P.D. were certain they had a serial killer on the loose. It was quiet for a year. Then came an additional preteen girl. All the patterns held similarities to Pearl's case. All of those girls were found this spring. A construction crew unwittingly dug up the first body breaking ground for a new neighborhood that was once a thriving tobacco field. In the ensuing week, investigators identified the skeletal remains of the other two buried in the same field.

Loose ties to each case had always been apparent to the Pruitt family, who sold adjacent land to their farm to an out-of-state developer years beforehand. Going through what the farmer described as a financial crisis—the cost of growing tobacco had outpaced the demand from cigarette manufacturers, payments shrank, and flood damage from two concurrent hurricane seasons meant the other crops never made it to market— the Pruitts were too distracted to ponder on other's troubles and chalked the entire situation up to coincidence.

When the Pruitts turned their son in, the patriarch described it as an eerie six degrees of separation. Though, if anything at all, it was more like two or three degrees if you included the suspect's parents. Aware he was about to be arrested, Franklin Pruitt hung himself in his parents' barn.

Mrs. Turner was the only parent of those four girls who never had her child's remains returned. Since Pearl was the first of the girls to go missing, Mrs. Turner contacted me, adamant that Franklin Pruitt had a direct connection to Pearl's case. She was resolute that the only people who knew the truth were deceased.

Despite forewarning Susan Turner about getting hustled by a clairvoyant, and the legalities of the "proof" they uncover, she'd poured her remaining hope into psychic intuition.

But wasting department resources, and allowing a woman like Rae Lee to disrupt the Turners' lives for nothing, is a mistake I'll pay for. So I hope to hell it never slips that I was stupid enough to have let my defenses down and fucked her. My credibility is screwed if it slips that, after the amazing way she deep-throated me, I was the sucker who used my cock to make sure the experience was reciprocal.

I'm a cop. I should know better than to fall for a pretty face.

"Was someone with Pearl?" Mrs. Turner grabs Rae Lee's hand, pleading for more information.

Wrapped up in her own emotions, Mrs. Turner doesn't observe Rae Lee wobbling or the paleness of the medium's cheeks. Not even the strobe lights from the stage washed Rae Lee out as much.

Great. I've endured my coworker's non-stop ribbing. Agreeing to this silly request has made me a laughingstock at the station. All I need when I write up my report is for the psychic to have passed the fuck out.

It's easier to lie to myself that the only benefit to me caring if this woman feels well is because of the monkey wrench it'll throw in the investigation. It eases the heat scorching my collar—a blaze that erupted when her delicate foot emerged from that

Uber. The foot that's connected to the supple calve I stroked last night, committing it to memory to use the next time I was alone.

I know Rae Lee heard Mrs. Turner's straightforward question, but her expression is puzzling. Her left eye opens and shuts as if she has something in it. It's weird how she concentrates on Pearl's mother's side, trying to regain her composure. Rae Lee waits to speak until Mrs. Turner drops her hand.

"I don't know who she was with. It was a dare. That's all Pearl keeps saying. Emphatically. And she's showing me water. Like a fountain. There are pennies at the bottom..." Rae Lee's fingertips flutter around me in a circle. "There's cement and walkways that come out. Like this and this." Her hands swish, crossing to her front, back, and sides. "And then there's grass and some trees in the distance, but not far, far away. Lots of kids go there. Families. Pearl plays with the kids sometimes. And then after dark she goes back under the ground." Rae Lee points downward. "Maybe under the fountain? I feel..." The psycho—*sorry, psychic*—rubs her fingertips together. "Dirt. Crumbly dirt. Like sand?" She brushes her skirt. "It's dirty, and it's on my clothes and in my hair. On my face." Rae Lee wipes it away, even though there's nothing there.

"What happened between Pearl leaving and the water?" I watch steam billow from her ears.

"I can't see it. She won't show me. It's like she

was upset, but the fear didn't happen until... It was too late? And maybe..." Rae Lee scratches her head, moving a lock of blonde hair that keeps falling out of place. My fingers itch to smooth it down and tuck it behind her ear to match how she wears it with the tips curling upwards at her shoulders.

"Maybe?" Mrs. Turner prompts.

"She doesn't want you to know her final moments. She says it was painful for you when her dad died... It's almost like keeping it from you is a layer of protection?"

I refrain from coughing in my hand and uttering a gravelly "bullshit".

A dead girl protecting her mother from knowing who her murderer was is as preposterous as anything else that Rae Lee has said to me in the past eighteen hours. Because of her stupid dirt pantomime, it feels like Rae Lee hasn't given us anything solid to go on.

I decide to wrap it up. Mrs. Turner's anguish is palpable. Mr. Turner's restless shadow keeps popping into view as he skulks in another room, waiting for permission to rejoin us. And above all else, sacrificing a good night's sleep for a regrettable fuck has shortened my fuse.

Before Rae Lee leaves, Mrs. Turner profusely thanks her for coming. I take another few minutes to comfort Mrs. Turner. Concern for his wife apparent, Mr. Turner holds her close and asks me if the medium gave me anything to go on.

"Not a lot," I admit. "But you never know what clues can reopen a case." I placate the couple. "If anything changes, I'll be in touch."

Mrs. Turner asks if she can contact Rae Lee directly. I check my suit pockets for my cell and AirDrop the contact card to the Turners.

Grifting is probably how Rae Lee Chatham makes money, anyhow. Why not cut out the middleman, save me the hassle, and the department the expense?

After how long the goodbyes took, I'm surprised to see Rae Lee still outside. She cautiously lowers herself to the curb. A feat in the tight skirt she's wearing. She stretches her legs out into the road.

"Don't get run over," I say, striding towards my car.

She glances over her shoulder. "I'll take my chances. Thanks. My other choice is giving all the neighborhood pervs a view of my panties."

"Standing is an option."

She wiggles her phone at me. "My ride is running late. I made the mistake of not eating, and since I'm woozy, I'd prefer not cracking my skull open and making that lovely woman's day any worse than I already did." She pauses. "For what it's worth, I planned to tell you I was sorry."

"When?" I ask curtly.

The question stings like a slap across her face. "When I got here."

"No. I mean, when did you know I was who you were meeting today?"

Her eyes dart from me to the gravel road and back again. "I knew for sure when I saw your badge in the kitchen." She rolls her lips, then admits, "But it's not as if I didn't intentionally avoid asking."

Sincere remorse mars her features. I'm certain that's the only honest thing she's said to me.

"Why didn't you?"

"Because the way you reacted to meeting *Raleigh* yesterday is the opposite of how you reacted to meeting Rae Lee today. Haven't you ever felt the pull to be someone you're not, Detective Ames? To leave it all behind just for a few hours?"

Chapter Four

Anson

Expecting I have nothing more to contribute to the conversation, Rae Lee doesn't seek a response. She directs her attention anywhere but at me.

I drink in her profile. Her pert little nose. The shape of her eyebrow over a big blue eye. There had been something undeniable about her heart-shaped face when we glimpsed one another at the bar. That, for as alluring as she was, Raleigh's closed-off expression meant her interest lay in a single night. She wouldn't linger in my bed. Wouldn't anticipate us exchanging numbers. Wouldn't expect flowers or a dinner date… And the air of mystery about her allowed me to turn her into a fantasy that fulfilled my needs.

I pretend I still have something that makes my life worthwhile besides the dedication to the force.

Whenever anyone forces me to admit I don't, I become fixated on my anger. One of the few things able to help me emerge from the depths is tossing a ball around in the backyard with Angeline's son. Although even the kid has a girlfriend and he's begun pestering me about why I don't.

An odd sense of *déjà vu* washes over me. It's similar to what I felt when I asked Rae Lee to my place last night: not being ready to let go of her. The overwhelming desire to spend a few more hours in Rae Lee's company takes charge, protesting my rationality.

"Cancel the ride. I'm taking you to get something to eat." I open the passenger side door.

"Why?"

"Because after all that, I can't leave you on the curb, disturbing what little peace the Turners still have."

Also, if something happens to her, nobody is pinning it on me that I left Rae Lee here. She could get run over. Or the ride share driver is a psycho who wants her for his collection. I'm a cop, worst-case scenarios fill the empty spaces in my mind.

She grudgingly stands and wipes the grass off her bottom. We ride in silence, making the trek to the lunch car diner feel longer than it takes.

Inside, a waitress escorts us to a booth and brings over two waters. At my insistence, Rae Lee orders a club sandwich. Toasted rye, mustard, light mayo, and the pickle to the side. She won't add a soft drink, which sticks me as odd because we're being bombarded with retro-styled Cheerwine advertisements decorating the prefabricated walls and Pepsi sponsors the menu boards above the counter.

I order a cup of coffee for now and a cinnamon bun to go. I'm not hungry. The pastry is meant to relax Rae Lee, so she doesn't notice she's the only person eating and perhaps, if I'm lucky, let me in on what she thinks she saw. I'll have it for dessert tonight.

The psychic groans, pressing the on button to wake her phone to no avail. "Stupid battery is forever draining itself."

"Carry a charging brick."

"I used to. Those drain just as fast."

"Maybe you should make sure they're both fully charged before leaving the house." She's a psychic. Didn't she see this coming?

Rae Lee blinks at me. The gears in her mind turn a sarcastic combination of "why didn't I think of that" and "duh, you idiot."

Which is what I am for believing a liar. Apparently, I'm also a sucker because she has no way to call for another ride and that leaves me chauffeuring her home.

The waitress drops off my coffee. I empty a sugar packet into the mug. Rae Lee still hasn't spoken when the spoon I've stirred with creates a soggy brown stain on a paper napkin. "What brought you out last night that made you feel you couldn't be yourself?" I lift the cup to sip. "I'm not judging."

"Then what are you doing?"

"Trying to understand how the woman I took to bed last night wound up being the medium I contacted to try to answer Mrs. Turner's prayers."

She sighs. "My cat died."

I blink and place my mug back on the laminate table. That's not what I expected to hear from Rae Lee at all.

"Your cat?" I scoff.

"*Mm-hmm…* Your turn, Detective. Unless picking up random strangers is part and parcel for you? I'm not judging either. I just don't really want to know that what's got your panties in a wad isn't that you feel duped. It's that I'm hookup number ten this month, and now you're worried about what happens when numbers one through nine march into this diner and ruin your upstanding reputation."

"You'd rather carry on the fairy tale that you're number one?" I lean against the Naugahyde seat back, threading my fingers over my stomach.

She shrugs. At first, I think she's indifferent to my opinion of her. Except then she leans forward and says, "You know, being the way I am isn't a day in the fucking park. I've dealt with judgmental as fuck people who think I'm a fraud all my life. So seriously, fuck you right up your dry fucking ass for trying to slut shame me when you're obviously as big a fucking whore as you're trying to make me out to be. You're the only fucker I've fucked lately and thank fuck for that. I didn't ask for, or need, your chauvinistic shit."

My brows raise and my lips pinch, taking the beating down I deserve. In her shoes... Nah, I *am* just as angry that her first impression of me is that I'm a manwhore.

Silence fills the air. Rae Lee grabs her things to go. Not that I blame her. I hadn't given her much of a chance before we met, so my reaction to her intentional miscommunication is the way I'd treat a habitual offender. I open my mouth, intending to make amends with a lackluster sorry. I mean, who cares that this woman got it wrong and casual sex isn't my norm? I'll probably never see Rae Lee Chatham again.

That's what you thought before.

"This week marks the anniversary of the death of someone I loved," I blurt.

Weirdly enough, Angeline used Rae Lee for a case. It's what prompted me to pick up the phone to call her when Mrs. Turner was insistent we'd find her daughter buried in the neighborhood like the other girls.

"Drinking to forget is a common bond." The faint smile I'm treated to is the same as the one with a hint of sorrow that crossed her face when I got her name wrong.

"So you *were* drowning your sorrows at Sweet Caroline's?" I confirm.

"More like drowning out the noise."

My forehead pinches, not understanding.

"Paul, my cat, was sick. It was finally his time.

But animals don't show themselves to me. I don't have whatever that ability is." She flicks her wrist. "When my defenses go down, everyone gloms on. They take advantage of my sadness, wanting to be heard, and I don't really want to listen." She makes a slashing movement. "Like sometimes I need them to cut it out."

I want to ask if she means dead people, but of course she does.

I've been a cop for a long time. I've encountered a lot of individuals who, right or wrong, are convinced the unexplained equates to the paranormal. Their unwavering conviction that it cannot be anything else is mind-blowing. They accept it as God's honest truth. So what if it seems like an act? My reluctance to accept Rae Lee's "gift" doesn't make it any less true for her. What it will do is keep putting her on the defensive. She won't mention any details she omitted, and without specifics, the Turners don't get their answers.

Our waitress delivers Rae Lee's sandwich. I let her chew and swallow a few bites before bringing up the things that bugged me during her walk.

"Why were you glad the Turners didn't have any more children?" My hands splay on the table, an open plea for her to be honest.

"I didn't say that." She wipes her mouth.

"You did."

Even if it wasn't my job, after fucking it up last night, I'd been paying close attention this morning.

Her relief was palpable when Rae Lee said "oh, good."

I kick my chin up. "Why would you wish for the Turners to remain childless? Was there something, some sort of sign?" I somehow refrain from rolling my eyes.

Rae Lee washes down the next bite with water. She leans back in her seat. The rigidness of her posture isn't lost on me. Her arms straighten and she clutches her hands between her knees. "Listen, I can only go on what the dead show me. Everyone has their own reality, even them. They project the truth of the life they led. My experience with the dead has taught me to tread lightly. I'm uncertain if the emotions they portray are real or their interpretations of their traumas."

"But you think something happened to the kid… Beforehand."

"I don't know for certain."

"But if you took a wild guess? Isn't that what you do? Make your best assumption."

"I go on what they show me and how they make me feel."

"And how did Pearl make you feel about Mr. Turner?"

Clearly uncomfortable, Rae Lee studies the empty parking space outside the window. She rubs a hand from the side to the front of her neck. It drops to her lap and then she's clutching her middle. "Pearl doesn't trust him."

"Did he touch her? Inappropriately?"

"I can't be sure." Her words are quiet. "I had an

awareness. A prickling sensation on my inner thighs. One that a kid shouldn't know about. If anything happened, it was when she was younger." Rae Lee regards me with unease.

"I'll check into it." Though I doubt the initial investigation left a stone unturned.

"But how do you prove a child's been molested when she's presumed dead and he's cleared of suspicion? It's tangential. A fragment of her past. And while it is relevant to Pearl—"

"It's irrelevance to finding out what happened to her was problematic. So you sent Turner away."

"Pearl wasn't going to talk to me. This little girl is trapped between wanting her mommy and feeling like... like Mrs. Turner took Mr. Turner's side. She's too angry when her mother's new husband is in the room and she's set on hurting Harvey and Susan."

I cock a brow. Is Rae Lee trying to tell me that the ghost of a missing twelve-year-old is responsible for her mother's miscarriages?

"The dead show me things that living people find hard to believe. Things that are hard to describe. Sort of like how, for you, the emotion of crime comes together almost indescribably at the scene."

I wipe my palm over my forehead. "Yeah, I get it." Even in photographs, the brutality can be beyond comprehension if you don't have the full picture.

I share what I'm comfortable Rae Lee knows about Pearl's case—most of which she could glean from the internet. "She's the only victim her age from around the same time frame we haven't found. Are you certain it isn't possible the same guy murdered all four girls?"

"Yes. Franklin Pruitt didn't take Pearl."

"How did you come to that conclusion?"

"In previous situations, I've seen more than one person. The deceased I'm being asked to contact tell me they aren't 'alone'." Rae Lee holds up finger quotes. "They present themselves to me along with a consciousness, a perception, of the other victims. Or their killer, if the person who murdered them has also passed. You said the guy responsible for killing those three other girls died by suicide. Either they would've been with Pearl today or he would've made himself known. Oppressively. So I don't think the cases are linked."

"Are you positive?"

"No, but as much as I can be. What I do is instinctual. I'm not an idiot. I know what I discover isn't admissible in a court of law, but my findings are similar to police work. Don't you ever go with your gut?" she asks rhetorically.

"Yeah… and most recently, it led me astray."

"No disrespect, Detective Ames. But, if you're going to keep muttering beneath your breath about what happened between us, I'm going to be honest; I'm one hundred percent certain another part of your body led your decision-making last night."

I pick up my coffee and bring it to my lips to hide

the grin I can't help cracking at her cheek.

Chapter Five

Cautious not to spill, I take an overflowing bowl of strawberry shredded wheat to the table. If it sloshes, there's no one to lick up the sweetened milk anymore.

Paul was a senior cat when I adopted him during one of those events where the overflowing shelter waived the fees to place animals into new homes. I felt awful for Paul. The family he loved his entire life chose not to care for him in his old age.

I'd harbor less resentment and have more sympathy if it weren't for two reasons. The name on his cubby was "Cinnamon", which made me wonder if that was his original name at all or what the shelter volunteers picked for him. Reason number two was Paul was lethargic having just had his balls lobbed off. There's no accounting for how many litters Paul sired.

Talking about responsible pet ownership turns me into one of those Sally Struthers commercials on television when I was a little kid. Since Paul has been gone, I can practically hear Sarah McLachlan singing between my ears. My taut heartstrings are in danger of snapping.

I'm certain the heightened aggravation, believing humanity could do so much more for creatures who depend on them, is because I can't sense Paul at all. I don't know if he's living his best kitty afterlife. It makes me as normal as anyone else. The kind of ordinary I dream of. Yet, grieving like this is a hard pill to swallow.

I take a spoonful of cereal and pick up a smooth blue rock from the plastic snap case I sort stones into. The variegated blues with light swirls make me feel good. Good is a good feeling. Life isn't easy. You should take in the good whenever you can. It rolls into my palm. I wrap my fingers around the coolness and succumb to the pleasure of its weight, soaking in the joy beauty brings.

Setting it on the tray next to the silver wire and the pliers, I scoop another bite. A knock interrupts the spoon's flight to my mouth. My attention flies to the door, where I stored the leftover cat supplies until I could bring them to the shelter. Alongside, I donated the entire fee from Brighton PD in Paul's memory. Although I haven't seen a dime yet, and with the cost of his last veterinary visit, I might wind up short this month.

"Come in," I call.

A cascade of wavy brown hair precedes Layla's face when she pops her head into my loft. "How d'you know it's me?"

"Sixth sense," I say wryly. Layla and I have this conversation a lot. Her next remark will be along the lines of—

"What if I were an ax murderer?"

I roll my eyes, laughing. "Ax murderers rarely knock on my door at ten in the morning during the middle of the week."

Layla's visits are like clockwork on the days she doesn't work at Paisley's Boutique on the cute little main drag downtown. She and her fiancé, Julian, are my landlords. They live in the largest apartment. It takes up most of the ground floor. Their front door is the original entrance. The ornately carved banisters in the foyer lead up to the bedrooms. She has access to the neat bits of an old mansion that get taken for granted, like dumbwaiters and the corridor that leads to servant quarters.

That's what my loft is, the former housekeeper's digs. The lengthy room is bare bones in comparison. My kitchenette has an old spindly legged enamel sink with the built-in drainboard in garish contrast to the modern refrigerator. But I couldn't love the dousing rainwater head when I shower in the bathroom's clawfoot tub with the wraparound curtain any less.

Layla closes the door and comes over to sit at the

small round table. "How are you doing?" Her head tilts to the right where Paul used to nap in a ray of sunshine whenever I took out my jewelry making supplies.

"Sad but otherwise good," I answer directly.

"Yay, going out helped! Julian saw you dancing." She waggles her brows.

When Layla found out Paul crossed the rainbow bridge, she'd told Julian. He manages the talent at Sweet Caroline's and, weeks earlier, had mentioned the lineup at the concert hall. I replied how I enjoyed several of them, and the one playing that night in particular. Later, I got a text from Julian saying, if I was up to go out, all I needed to do was drop his name at the door. The bouncer in turn asked my name, checked a list, told me to enjoy the show, and moved aside so that I could pass.

I'm a one-trick pony. The gal friends call to amuse themselves with my cool parlor tricks. Oftentimes, I'll hear nothing for months, until someone picks up the phone to call because they are grieving and need closure with a loved one. Don't get me wrong, in those instances, I want to help. However, the support Layla and Julian gave me, listening to what I needed and acknowledging that I grieve too, is rare.

Layla and Julian are also aware that I've stopped volunteering my services. The toll past readings have taken on my body is immense. But when the referral came from someone who knew Angeline, refusing was difficult. As a matter of fact, I'd agreed without a second thought. Within hours, Paul's health declined. Losing my companion right as I needed to shift my mindset and prepare to meet Pearl's mother was horrible timing.

My lips vibrate as I blow a breath out of the side of my mouth. "Yes, going out helped me relax. Except, I sort of did something I shouldn't have and blew it all to hell." I slump, my shoulder blades hitting the hard chair back.

"Something or someone?"

"The guy I sent the picture of me with was Anson Ames, the detective who called me to consult on that cold case." I study the painted-over cracks in the ceiling. "I sort of gave him a fake name, and now he doesn't believe anything I said during the investigation."

Layla's jaw hits the floor. "And here all I was wondering was if any ghosts followed you home."

Yes. But it's moot to mention since the dead haven't stayed. Out of desperation, I learned to keep barriers in place. I tell them they aren't welcome, and most of them go back to where they came from.

"I assume you..." I grab Layla's hands to stop her from making the lewd gesture. "I'll take that as a yes."

My cheeks flame. "Yes."

"Did he do a thorough investigation and make sure you got yours?"

"Yes!" I roll my eyes, laughing at Layla's directness.

She's the nearest thing I have to a confidant. A best friend. But on closer examination, it feels weird because Layla's an extrovert. Since moving to Brighton, she's made a million close associations through her boss, Paisley, who is engaged to Jake, Julian's boss and the owner of Sweet Caroline's. I hate leaching off of people or using up their energy because it's no fun to have an oddball loner dependent on their kindness. Still, I'm grateful Layla visits me so often.

"The man came to you about this case. Whenever anyone has begged you to do a reading there are always shallow non-believers nitpickers, or jerks who show up acting as if the open-minded friends who invited them are stupid. So who cares what Detective Ames thinks? If he thinks none of the information you gave him was any good, if he follows a lead and disproves it, then it's on him to report everything to his boss, not you

"And let's be real, you cannot be the first girl Anson has picked up at a bar who has given him a false name or wrong number." Layla fans her fingers. "Hell, the digits I gave Julian when we met were for a restaurant I waitressed at that had gone out of business. He had to chase me down to get my real number. He had to prove he was interested in me, not just drunkenly sing a verse from an Eric Clapton song off-key that a million other guys had already tried to pick me up with." She lets out an exaggerated groan. "Anson was good to you in the sack, and he was professional towards you and the family at the walkthrough, yes?"

"Yes."

"Then what difference does it make if you never see this man again?"

Because as much as I didn't want to be me that night, I liked who he was. I think.

Anson should have left me and my dead cell phone sitting in the gutter, which is exactly how I expected him to react. But not only did he have the humanity to get me food at the diner before I passed out, he also had the professional courtesy to drop me off at my apartment afterwards, and he waited for me to get safely inside.

I've spent the past several days dwelling on every interaction we had. Overthinking whether my defensiveness was justified or if I was overcompensating with the barrage of fucks I let loose on Anson because I was oversensitive. Overstimulated. What if I hadn't been so prickly? Not that I'd behave like a doormat.

I've gotta move on and stop letting Anson live rent-free in my head. Angeline kept me in the loop, updating me on how her case unfolded after we worked together. Pearl's mother left a thank you in my voicemail. Anson had to have given Mrs. Turner my number. I haven't heard a thing from him, and it's going to remain that way.

I fiddle with a sealed cup of lobster claw clasps, unwilling to part with the answer on the tip of my tongue. The real me would've scared Anson off, but not letting him see who I really am did the same thing.

It's under my skin because I want more of something I can't have.

"I guess you're right," I begrudgingly admit. It doesn't make a difference because I won't hear from Anson Ames again.

"One last question: Was Detective Ames as hot as he looked in the picture?"

"Yes." I laugh, fanning my cheeks.

"Figured. The hot ones always leave scorch marks. Or beard burn." Layla shrugs with a wink.

She plucks a vibrant orange sunstone with a vein of red running through it from the open box of gemstones to admire. Then she moves the thick gauged wire and pliers onto my self-healing craft mat. "This color is selling out as fast as we're stocking it. Paisley wants more."

Chapter Six

Anson

"I've been meaning to ask..." Chaim, my superior officer, wiggles a pen over his desk. The ends hit his blotter, making a rapid *tick-tick-ticking*, and tiny ink stabs appear. "That psychic chick turn up any new leads?"

He stops, clicks the end, closing the pen, and chucks it into the holder. Then he pushes back in his chair. His ass doesn't do that balancing act in the seat. There's not enough room between his desk and the bookshelf cramped behind it to recline. It's more of a closet than an actual office. A place the powers that be stuck him because his years of service afford Chaim a level of privacy I haven't reached.

My desk is among the other detectives; homicide, narcotics, and computer crimes. When I have to walk down a hall for a face-to-face with Chaim, I stand the entire time since there's no room for a second chair in his hidey-hole.

The few of us—Okay, the *two* of us, Chaim and me—assigned to split Brighton P.D.'s unsolved missing persons and cold cases understand that, like any police department, we're understaffed and woefully under-funded. I mean, it's not as if we've got cement blocks tied to our legs and are swimming through unsolved murders. But it's something the Chief of Police claims they're aiming to change.

The public uproar after the Pruitt case was bad fucking press for the town of Brighton. Proof won out. Except, cameras and conjecture went unchecked. It left a lot of citizens under the impression that inept small-town cops assigned to cases over a decade ago are why those girls weren't found here sooner.

Not that every officer, in every town, who worked those cases doesn't have their own regrets. In hindsight, everyone is wondering how the victims remained hidden so close by. What evidence was missed. What anyone could have done better, differently, from the onset.

Reality is, even working with other jurisdictions, there wasn't the access to forensic experts or the advanced technologies we have today. Time marches on. Technology changes. States are working diligently to get the backlog of offender fingerprints and DNA samples from convicted felons into CODIS. The scope and the backlog of information are immense. But, with any luck, eventually searching those databases should crack remaining cases and stop many from going unsolved in the future.

Until then, we keep at it.

Chaim's and my time get split. The men and women we investigate ongoing crimes with are dedicated. They take pride each and every time they don't have to hand files off to us. Can you blame them for wanting to do great police work? I can't.

Not after Pruitt.

Leaning cross-legged against the doorjamb to his office, I grab my jaw with my thumb and forefinger, moving it back and forth to test how sensitive it is.

While I've kept what went down at Sweet Caroline's quiet, my life since meeting Rae Lee Chatham has been an utter disaster. I'd gone the following morning for a filling only for the dentist to discover the molar needed a root canal and crown. That afternoon, a private investigator in Goldsboro sidetracked me. Try as I may over the weekend, every time I sat on the couch to watch a game, my attention span vanished. All I could think of was the way Rae Lee's body felt against mine.

I think she put some voodoo hex on me because I lost the TV remote every time I put it down, and my phone and keys magically disappeared more than usual. Not to mention, this morning my laptop bag wasn't in the spot where I normally leave it in the kitchen. It somehow got tucked in the corner alongside my shoe rack at the door. *I never leave my computer by the door.* I wound up skidding into the dentist's parking lot, five minutes late for the root canal.

"Dhere's a few tings Chadham said that I'm foddowing up on. I need to ged on id."

I have better things to occupy my time than shooting the shit. Plus, whenever I open my mouth, my fat tongue and puffy lips have me slurring my words. I sound like a bumbling buffoon.

Chaim, who carried most of the conversation, chuckles at my speech. "Hope that novocaine wears off soon, man."

"Thdanks. Me tdoo." I turn to go.

"Wife's out of town. Wanna get dinner tonight? Liquid. If you can manage," Chaim calls. "Mark-39 introduced a new beer."

After the day I've had, a cold beer with a buddy sounds too good to be true. I also hope to have full use of my lips again by dinnertime and not dribble all over myself when I drink. I'm in.

I nod a hello to the people I pass in the hall, sit down at my desk, and sort through the notes I took from Rae Lee's reading at the Turners'.

I start where the likelihood of finding something concrete to go on is highest. Using my computer to search local parks, I get ten pages' worth of hits in Brighton and surrounding jurisdictions. Most of them are within the radius of the Pruitt farmland. I'll fan out if I need to expand the search as far as the capital.

I switch to satellite view. One by one, I zoom in and drag the screen around the perimeter of each playground to get an idea of the size, checking for the potential of anything hidden that I'd need to go investigate on foot. Then I move to the center of the park, looking for sidewalks or water features similar to what Rae Lee described.

Checking the first page of hits off my list takes me an hour. So far, I have one park where the trees obscured the view and the aspect on the street view hadn't stretched to show me what I needed to rule it out. I click to page two and continue.

The next park is oblong. It's within a stone's throw of an elementary school. Lush green pines circle out, surrounding a soccer field. Directly across the street is a baseball diamond. There's an entrance for a parking lot. But there's also a sidewalk that takes anyone there for recreation up to the playground equipment. It looks like there might be a second entrance I can't see through the foliage.

I drop my virtual self on the striped crosswalk. The avatar's view faces the baseball diamond. There's a pole for a solar-powered pedestrian crossing with a bucket of bright orange flags attached.

I click the right arrow on the screen. I see a school zone speed limit sign. There are no stoplights within the horizon. A large city park sign shows the turn into the parking lot. Then the sidewalk on the park side of the street seems closer. Slowly, I scroll farther to the right... And I can't believe my eyes.

I jump out of my seat so quickly that I bang the front of my thighs against the desk drawer.

Twenty minutes later, I pull my car into the lot. Rushing to the main entrance, incredulous at what I'm seeing. The street sidewalk is from side to side. The painted crosswalk lines merge with a path straight into the park. A few feet beyond where the two intersect is a wishing well that's about five feet in diameter and three feet tall. It's surrounded by a circular walkway. The water is shallow and still. A handful of pennies and nickels are scattered on the chipped blue bottom. It wouldn't surprise me if younger kids fed the well and the older ones took from it.

Does calling life as I see it make me jaded?

Parked off to the side of the walkway is a white two-seater utility vehicle with Town of Brighton Parks and Recreation splashed over the hood. Next to it is a dry-vac style pump with a corrugated tube snaking toward the well and an orange outdoor extension cord running the opposite way.

There's a tug on the extension cord. Seconds later, an older fellow in tidy coveralls pokes out. The shade doesn't hide the deep wrinkles on his forehead and around his eyes that he's earned from laboring in the sun. He has a white goatee and a pot belly concealed by his height and his uniform.

I approach him slowly, indicating I've read the name embroidered on his badge. "Morris?" I show him mine. "Detective Ames." I biff the S. "Sorry, root canal."

"I hear ya, boy. Had one of them myself. Just talk slow." He looks to see if anyone is around. "Be like me. Pretend *I* don't talk slow." He winks, tossing his head back with a raspy chuckle.

I'd classify Morris as a bit jaded, but his overall demeanor is jovial.

"I'm investigating a case. Do you mind answering a few questions?"

Carefree, Morris's pearly whites beam from ear to ear. He grunts his approval, slipping his hands into his pockets, and rocks back on his heels.

I speak slower, like he instructed me to. "You do the maintenance here?"

"I take care of this one and a few others."

"What can you tell me about the park?"

"Ain't much different from any other ol' park. Greenway. Playground. Field. Trees. Houses now all around it. 'Sides this backbreaker, they're all pretty much the same."

"You don't like wishing wells?"

"They never shoulda put this here. Stupidest place for a water feature ever, if ya ask me. It ain't even got anything to keep it full or the water circulating. And cleaning it is something awful. Bird poop. Kids leaving stuff in it. Gum. Candy wrappers. Food Wrappers. Sometimes worse."

Morris scrunches his nose. Experience has made him jaded, too. "I don't know whose bright idea it was. But it wasn't mine."

I take Morris to be efficient: a no-nonsense type of guy.

He moves toward the town vehicle, either tired of standing still or of my lackluster questions. Or maybe Morris has a job to do and the longer he flaps his gums, the longer it'll take to get it done and go home. I can't blame him for wanting to multitask.

"When did the city install it?" Again, mundane. I can search the town archives.

"I dunno. Fifteen, twenty years ago. Lost track." He widens his feet, spraying neon orange on the far edge of a slab that's raised so that no one trips. The opposite edge of the adjacent one has been ground down.

The tip of my shoe toes the wide vee in the middle of the two concert slabs. "What does this?"

"Makes the sidewalk uneven? Overgrown tree roots mostly." Morris lifts the hand holding the spray can to the leafy canopy. "Sometimes, the ground shifts when we get too much rain. Flooding and all. All the building they been doing means there's less place for the water to go, so it moves the earth tryina forge a new runoff trail." He points the nozzle at the wishing well. "Hurricane season is the only time that's ever full and it's to overflowing. Glad they're taking it out. Parents these days, their noses in their phones instead of watching their littluns. It's not safe. Not safe. Somebody's baby is going in headfirst and going to drown and somebody else is going to post that whole tragedy on their instacart for the whole world to see."

Instagram. But he has a point. Bystanders shooting a video first and calling for help second is becoming a frequent problem that puts lives at risk.

"You get a lot of animals around here?"

"Yep. *It's a park.* Squirrels. Possums. Raccoons love the trash cans. Deers. Did you know them and those coyotes are getting moved along by all these new houses?"

"What if something decomposed?" I cut Morris off.

"Yeah. It would have to be a big thing to cause a sinkhole. A stump or something or other." He drops the hose into the well.

"Do you know offhand how long it would take a stump to decay?"

"In this climate, if I were to guess... Three years?" He shrugs.

"How long has the sidewalk been buckling?"

"Pretty much since we put it in."

"And that was twenty years ago?"

Morris's face elongates. His head bobs from shoulder to shoulder. "It coulda been more like fifteen."

Fuck me, there's a chance Rae Lee Chatham might be on to something.

His finger hovers over the shop-vac, ready to push the on button. "Anything else?"

"That's it for now. Thank you."

I head to the parking lot, jumping as the vacuum loudly begins sucking the water out. Biting the inside of my cheek with a crunch, my eyes tear and I hold back the *Ow*.

"Hey, detective?"

I raise a brow, rubbing my sore face.

"If you've gotta camera, I'd be taking some pictures if you need any for your case. The park administrator finally did me a favor. I'm emptying this headache because it's getting torn out."

Chapter Seven

Anson

Back at the precinct, I place a call to the parks and recreation department. It goes to voicemail. I search the web, finding an article on the ribbon cutting for the well. The pictures show lots of children running on the sidewalks. A toddler tosses a coin into the well. The event was a month after Pearl disappeared. I run my hand through my hair, fisting chunks. Then I pick up the phone again.

This time I get a hold of the parks and rec admin. She'll pull what they have on the park's history and maintenance and send it tomorrow.

"Do you have employment records? Or anything about what company installed the wishing well?" I ask.

"We purge anything older than ten years. But

you might find it archived through the city clerk's office."

"Great." That's the next email I fire off. The city clerk likes a detailed message, so they don't have to do the work twice. Anytime I've called, they've asked me to put it in writing.

My inbox pings with a similar response to the parks and recreation department. They'll get on my request ASAP.

I know these things take time, but after what Morris mentioned about the well demolition, it feels like I'm wading in molasses. In an instant, finding out what happened to Pearl weighs on my shoulders. It's like the entire town of Brighton is right and I'm not doing what needs to get done fast enough.

In all honesty, I dealt with my grief the week preceding the anniversary of Angeline's death by giving her son all of my extra waking hours. I haven't been at my best because my cup was fucking empty when Mrs. Turner contacted me. I should've been more prepared for the meeting than I was. Humans make mistakes. I'd ask Mrs. Turner for her forgiveness if it didn't open a whole other can of worms.

What's more, the idea that I surreptitiously dismissed Rae Lee bugs the hell out of me. I later examined my bias towards her because of the lie she told. I'm aware my sisters have done the same thing. I'm the cop who suggested it for their safety.

Good god, I don't need the mental images of my

sisters having one-night stands. It's bad enough that thoughts of Rae Lee's lips around my cock and the way she rolled the condom over my shaft and sunk down on my dick have me half hard again. I've rubbed one too many out to the memory of her tits being pushed up by the bra, sucking on her pert nipples and the way her skin tasted. If she stayed, I intended on having a real taste of her. Instead, I woke up alone with a sour taste in my mouth. I'd even searched my apartment to make sure she hadn't stolen anything.

So yeah, I wasn't exactly kind when her heel hit the grass, and I doubt outside of the sandwich I bought her—big fucking spender that I am—I'll have the opportunity to make up for that.

The distraction makes it harder to concentrate. My buzzing cell gets lost under a file, and I miss an incoming text from Chaim. He's caught up in something and needs another hour before we hit Mark-39. Fine by me since it's taking me a year to find the file with the case's box number in the evidence locker. When I finally have it, I'm on my feet again, hustling to another part of the building.

Pearl's case hasn't had a break like the Pruitt murders. I have access to digitized crime scene photos and a list of the box's contents using my laptop. I wasn't with the department during the discovery phase, which necessitates ensuring I haven't inadvertently overlooked any of the evidence the detectives seized. Once I see the logbook, it's obvious no one has put eyes on it in quite a while.

Amongst the articles inside the box, I find a softball bat found underneath the bed on Pearl's floor and brown-stained green hand towel, presumably used to wipe the blood off of it. No prints were on either, which is odd since Pearl's bat should have Pearl's prints on it. Currently, getting decent prints off of a cotton textured towel is a challenge. I can't imagine it back then.

Having no body means Pearl's picture is in circulation using age progression. But if she's dead, in all probability, this is the murder weapon.

Did I imagine Rae Lee holding her head when we were at the Turner's? I need to ask her if she saw how Pearl died.

Why do you believe this woman? I ask myself. *What besides your pride is stopping you from believing her?* I answer.

I put everything back in the box and go back to my laptop on my desk to open the forensics file. I scroll through the list of items, mentally checking them off in my head. Then I flip over the DNA collection sheets.

Pearl's to match the blood on the towel.

Mrs. Turner's.

Mr. Turner's.

Wait.

Why did the original investigator swab Harvey Turner when they'd already matched the blood to Pearl?

My eyes bug out reading the pathologist's report.

Semen found on the towel was a one hundred percent match to Mr. Turner.

I search through the investigation notes and find an answer. But it's been a long time and I want it from the horse's mouth.

"Mr. Turner. Detective Ames. I'm doing some follow-up on the investigation and was hoping to ask you a few questions," I say when Mrs. Turner's new husband answers the phone.

"They're about the towel," he replies succinctly.

"Yes, they are."

"Like I told the first detective, Pearl interrupted Susan and I when we were…and *uh,* you know how it goes. I finished in the bathroom. It was the closest thing to grab to get the job done."

"This happened the day Pearl disappeared?"

"Yes. Susan and I had been waiting for Pearl to get back from her friend Ellen's. Susan was unsure we'd have any privacy after going out to dinner. Pearl had a habit of rushing me out of the house. I thought we had more time. She always lollygagged coming home."

"Why's that?"

"Losing her dad was just hard on Pearl. She had all those preteen hormones. Had a rough time with Susan dating. Moving on. It was almost like I was taking her mother away. Is there anything else?"

"Did you put it at the top or the bottom of the hamper?" I stare at the picture on my computer screen. The towel in the photograph is on top of girl's clothing.

"Not the bottom. But not on top. I used the bathroom Pearl used. I hadn't wanted her to find it."

My curiosity is piqued. I know the Turners have a master bathroom. Who hadn't Harvey wanted to find the towel with his jiz? Was it Pearl... or Susan?

"Thanks for your continued cooperation, Mr. Turner. If there is anything else, I'll let you know." I hang up the phone.

Aside from a crime going unsolved, something doesn't feel right. There are pieces that don't fit together, and I don't know if pursuing Turner is a wild goose chase.

"Hey, you ready?" Chaim taps me on the shoulder.

"Yeah, *uh*, no. Rain check on me. I need to—" I flash a finger at my laptop.

"I get it." Chaim backs away with a "been there" attitude. "Don't stay too late."

"I won't. In the morning, I need your expertise on a search warrant."

"You have probable cause?"

"Exigent circumstances. Destruction of Evidence." Reasonable suspicion aside, I want the wording spot on so that I can be there when the town removes the wishing well.

"Type it up and send it over. Sure you don't want a beer? I'm still buying."

"I'm sure."

I spend the next hour tracking down Ellen

Wainstraw, Pearl Tatton's best friend from middle school. She agrees to meet me.

"Did Pearl ever give you the impression that she was afraid of Mr. Turner?" I ask Ellen the following day.

Ellen's lower jaw juts out, her teeth scraping her upper lip. I patiently wait for her to speak. "I don't think I thought she was afraid of him, but she didn't like that Susan was having a relationship with him."

"Did Pearl tell her mother she didn't want her mother dating him?"

"I guess her mom knew. Susan stopped seeing Harvey for a while."

"How long?"

Ellen exhales. "Six months? Maybe more. It was a long time ago, but I don't remember not knowing Pearl didn't want Harvey around. She didn't like him even before her dad died."

"Was she afraid of him?" I rephrase the question, trying a second time. I hate to lead anyone to conclusions, but I suspect from Ellen's first answer that she hadn't realized her best friend might have had something to fear. "Can you recall a situation where Pearl expressed any apprehension about being left alone with Mr. Turner?"

"Not one situation. A lot of them." Ellen looks to the sky. "You know all the Pinewood State news coverage, detective?"

"Of course." If the station weren't abuzz with my co-workers keeping abreast with the developments as the perp went to trial, the news reports would have been hard to miss.

"My sorority sister was one of the victims." Ellen glances down, her cheek pulls in. The young woman tears up.

"I'm sorry to hear that. Is your friend getting the help she needs?" I have contacts I'm glad to offer.

"Yes, she is. Thank you. It's been a rough road for her. I—*ugh*, I've never known anyone who was assaulted, raped, or... I don't know, I thought I didn't."

"Now you aren't sure."

"We were twelve. Like when I got my first period and my mom had to have the talk with me... I was still trying to wrap my head around adults doing *that*. That my parents would do that. A man doing those things to a kid? It just never crossed my mind. I never thought the reason Pearl had anything against her dad's business partner was because he'd, you know, done those kinds of things to her."

"But since the Pinewood State rape trial, you can't stop thinking he could have."

Ellen nods, her lips twist. She dabs her eyes with her sleeve. "It was so hard for my sorority sister and we weren't kids. Her soul was crushed, and it affects everything she wants to do for the rest of her life."

She covers her face, composing herself. "How could that happen to a little girl? What kind of monster would do that to his friend's daughter? To the child of a woman he was dating? I feel like I have to be wrong about it, Detective Ames. That Pearl would have told me. Flat out told me why she hated Harvey. We were best friends. I would have kept her secret."

I give Ellen a hug and a gentle pat on the back. "That's never a secret a child should keep."

Chapter Eight

Rae Lee

My thumb hovers over the decline button. I want to send Anson Ames to voicemail for ignoring me. But I also can't stop thinking about if he's gotten a break in Pearl's case. Or, if I'm honest, the night we spent together.

"If it's important, take it." Paisley notices my hesitation.

"Thanks," I say, appreciating her understanding. My next breath is an airy "hello" that boldly contradicts having no desire to be at his beck and whim.

"Rae Lee." He gets down to business. "Anson Ames. You wouldn't have a few minutes to go over your investigation again, would you?"

"I'm sorry. I'm delivering some products at Paisley's Boutique downtown."

"How long will you be?"

"Another half hour or so. I can call you back when I'm finished."

"How about I meet you outside the shop in forty-five? I'd like to talk in person. I'll even throw in dinner."

I peer down at the breezy pattern on my flowing skirt, the solid V-neck tee. I've paired the outfit with cute wedge sandals with the braided thong and silver charm that I purchased on clearance at the upscale shop. Luckily, I specifically chose something a notch above yoga pants and a hoodie to come in and drop off my wares. So I agree to meet Anson underneath the awning outside when I'm finished.

A half an hour passes, and Anson is already pacing the sidewalk. He concentrates on his phone screen. The jeans he's wearing fit him like a glove, and the dark button-up stretches over his broad back the way his polo had when we met.

"Oh, is that him?" Layla sidles up behind me. "He's divine."

Staying to chat with my friend, I finger the lush fabric of some clothes on the center racks. I'm pretending I'm engaged in entrepreneurial activities, when in reality Layla's giving me a you-go-girl pep talk. She says I can handle whatever Hottie McCop dishes out this evening, though beneath my skirt my knees are knocking.

I rarely care about a man's opinion. So needing him to respect my gift and... well, me, because we have been intimate… is unusual.

A tinkling bell alerts Anson that I'm leaving the shop.

"Hey. Hi," he greets me, stuffing his phone in his jeans. "Up for Mark-39? My boss told me they have a new beer on draft."

"That's fine."

The pub is just up the street. Their pulled pork is a barbecue lover's dream, and they have every imaginable topping on the menu to build your own loaded fries.

On the way inside the restaurant, I show Anson a picture of a B-52 in flight. "I went to high school here and didn't realize that North Carolina had a nuclear mishap in the 1960s until this place opened. They still haven't found the bomb." My jaw drops, still incredulous. How do you lose an H-bomb? I'm glad they found the second one that the plane dropped as it broke up.

"A kid I get takeout for from here for told me that story. Are you a history buff?" he asks.

"Not at all." If I were, I would have paid closer attention. Some teacher must've mentioned it in class.

"What were you doing at Paisley's?" Anson asks after we're seated.

"Am I here for you to interrogate me, detective?"

"Making conversation." He shoots me a wide, toothy grin. "Our previous meal together wasn't a get-to-know-you, and we didn't talk much at Sweet Caroline's."

Heat creeps at my neck. The only things Anson said to me in between were dirty. I think about what he and I did constantly.

"I create one-of-a-kind jewelry." I roll my eyes and shake my head, shaking it off. "My landlord works for Paisley and showed her my website. Paisley decided to stock some of the wrapped crystals and gemstone necklaces." I hold the oblong sunstone around my neck up. "The store was out of stock on concentration bracelets—they're made of stones that sort of ground you. Some people use them as prayer beads. Others just like the way they look. I'd also gotten a request from her for more sunstone and wanted to balance that out by offering Paisley some moonstone before posting those online."

"This is what you do for a living?"

"It keeps me busy. Helps pay the bills. I'm not really cut out for anything else. And if I make too much money, I lose my disability benefits."

"I'm not trying to be mean, but you seem young and healthy."

"I was diagnosed with Rheumatoid Arthritis in my early twenties. I'd also been taking medication for migraines when I lost my balance and fell at work. Got a concussion. The ER doctor ordered a bunch of new tests and come to find out the stiff joints were fibromyalgia."

"I'm sorry."

"I am and I'm not. I don't have to make excuses for falling asleep anymore or explain why I'm having problems sleeping." My day is what I make of it. I rest when I need to and stay awake as long as I can manage. "I just wish I understood what I was doing to my body sooner."

"What do you mean?"

"When Angeline was alive, I did a lot of consulting. And even more readings. The kind you'd expect in a big room filled with people: dead and alive. Opening yourself up like that takes a toll. I wasn't smart about it." I hadn't built good barriers dealing with the dead, and it drained me.

"I think I used my abilities to gain acceptance. It backfired and instead I became the friend no one wanted to hang around with because her spooky powers and crazy health problems were more than they could deal with." I wiggle my fingers in the air like I'm casting a spell. I'm certain Anson believes this is all woo-woo, anyhow.

"That must bother you?"

"I live a quiet life, detective. Having fewer people to count on might not appeal to anyone else, but quality over quantity is good for me, and in my book, that's what counts."

We order. A burger and beer for him. Beer and steak fries topped with sirloin, salsa verde, and cheese for me.

"You're going to share those, right?" Anson drools when the waiter leaves us alone at our table.

I shouldn't notice him licking his lips after his first sip of beer. He glances at me over the rim of his pilsner glass, holding my lingering attention.

Those thick lashes entrance me again. I notice his pupils dilate.

Don't fool yourself, Rae Lee. This restaurant has low lighting.

"During the walkthrough, did Pearl tell or show you anything about a head injury?" Anson clears his throat, knocking me back to reality. He takes his phone back out to jot down what I say.

I cup my temple. "I had a hot, sticky sensation here. My vision got fuzzy, like blood was trickling into my eyes and blinding me."

"What about Mr. Turner? Can you run me through that again? Were there any other indications that you had that he might've sexually abused her?"

He continues taking notes, but most of what I recount seems redundant and counterproductive to what Anson needs to solve the case.

"I'm not sure any of this has been helpful." I frown, fisting my skirt under the table.

"It has. I've actually been tracking some leads."

"You have?"

"I met with Pearl's best friend, and today a judge signed off on a warrant. I can't give you any more details than that since it's an ongoing investigation. But both things are encouraging. I planned to tell you, we hadn't gotten that far in the conversation."

"What I saw helped?" Butterflies zoom in my belly.

"It absolutely did." He leans in and whispers,

"You might've made me a believer."

The server brings our food, and the table grows quiet. I pick at my plate of fries. Anson's confession makes me antsy. Grasshoppers spring off my insides, tickling me along with the butterfly wings. I want to know more about him. And maybe I'm curious about what's kept him from keeping me apprised.

"Do you date?" *Why did I ask that?* "I, uh, I got the impression that you and Angeline were involved."

"We'd dated some."

"Was it serious?"

"It would've gotten there, eventually. Angeline's divorce had just been finalized. We were… Taking it slow. She'd had a rough couple of years and her primary concern was her son, Grant."

Mothers put up with a lot of crap for their kids. Mine still does. But when I was a kid, my mom's patience ended with another adult messing with me. Angeline was the same. Deep down, I firmly believe Angeline understood her situation would only get worse. Yet, like most women, she hadn't wanted to give up on someone she once loved. I remember the news reports about the fallen officer. Angeline took her power back when Grant's father's threats became physical toward their son.

"I'm sorry for your loss." I offer my sympathy.

Anson shrugs. I think he's resigned, past the heartache, until his lips flatten and his chin pebbles.

"I'm sorry for Grant. Angeline was a great cop

and a wonderful mom. I've done what I can so that the kid has a guy in his life. But Grant lost out on having an actual parent when his dad was convicted."

"You think they could have co-parented, even with the domestic abuse?"

"I think… I think Grant deserves someone in his corner, and I try to be that person."

"You want kids?"

"Not anymore. You?"

"Not really. Not if they have to go through what I do."

"How did you find out you were like… this?" His palms open wide, hovering over the tabletop.

I lean back, sliding my hands between my knees. "I was four when I realized something was off. My nana couldn't live alone after my papa died and moved in with my parents before I was born. She took care of me while they worked."

"You must've been close."

The uncontrolled huff, little laugh, and smile bubble up, ringing out from a place deep inside of me. "We were. She was frail, but still got on the floor to play. Nana had a cough she couldn't shake, but no one seemed concerned. My parents went out for dinner. Nana baked me chicken nuggets and fries. After I finished eating, she'd told me to go color. I had a desk and a chair. It was about yay high." I gesture, measuring the level. "Nana took the phone into her bedroom and came back out a few minutes later. She sat down in her recliner, watching me choose what crayon I'd color with next. She said that I was a good girl, that Mommy and Daddy would be home soon, and that I shouldn't worry."

I wasn't afraid. Nana's face had been pinched while she was scraping my plate. I thought she was angry with me for wasting so much ketchup. But then she was happy. Smiling. I stopped worrying that I'd done something naughty by squeezing the bottle too hard. I felt like she was proud of me for trying to be a big girl."

"When my parents came home, my dad walked past Nana. My mom was hiding her panic—not very well. She asked where Nana was. But when I turned to say she was right there, Nana was gone. My dad found her in her bedroom, clutching the phone to her chest. She'd called them instead of 911."

"Wow. I'm… Speechless. Did you have any other experiences as a kid?"

"All sorts. Everything from knowing bad things were about to happen to being approached by people others couldn't see. Sometimes, friends would ask me why I was talking to myself. You can only find so many excuses before they label you and decide they don't want to hang out with a weirdo anymore. I'm glad for the invent of wireless earphones."

"Because now everyone looks like they are talking to themselves and everyone around them assumes they're talking on the phone," Anson supplies with a grin.

"You got it."

Chapter Nine

Anson

"Hold on, you really had a boyfriend named Ben Dover?" I jog around the hood of my car to catch up to Rae Lee, who is standing on the lawn.

"Yes." Rae Lee's goofy grin breaks into a snort. "No. I had you going there." She doubles over laughing as if we've had one too many at dinner.

I'm aware that's not it. Rae Lee and I each had two beers and a full dinner. I'd stolen her fantastic fries, and we split dessert when she saw pineapple upside down cake on the menu. The classic taste is evocative, reminding me of Sunday family dinners when I was a kid. Rae Lee mentioned licking the spatula when her nana baked it in a blue cornflower Corningware dish was one of her earliest recollections.

Once you break past her outer shell, Rae is silly.

She can say the absurd with a straight face, though it cracks as soon as she's got your number. The silliness, merriment, and the way she relaxes when she delivers the punchline for a joke makes her light up.

"Okay. You got me." The rumble of laughter that comes from deep within my belly takes me off guard. I hold my hands up in surrender. Neither of us are in control of our riotous smiles.

I should admit to Rae Lee that she has me entranced. No matter what I believed about her abilities before, I hadn't gotten her out of my mind. Helping people is serious business. Her method is simply unconventional. But I sorta like that she can break free of it and not take herself too seriously.

We shut down Mark-39. It's late and both of us have work tomorrow. Well, I do. Not that Rae Lee's circumstances bug me now that she's shared about her health issues. For the second time, we've had the kind of fun together that neither of us wants to end.

I grab her hand and pull her towards the back door that she used to enter the older house the first time I dropped her at home.

The night we met, I was attracted to a pretty woman, who simply wanted what I did—a good time. Raleigh was sexy and seductive. Rae Lee is beautiful and intelligent. She's also mysterious. Yet something tells me I wouldn't have to dig too much further to find out she has a heart of gold.

It's a stroke of luck that the two women I find so alluring are wrapped up in the same package.

Even though I shouldn't, I place my hand on her waist. Rae Lee looks down at her skirt where I'm touching her. The streetlamp makes her blush appear deeper.

"I'd invite you upstairs, but I think we both know where that leads." Her lip catches between her teeth.

"I'm not offended." I still can't sit on my couch without thinking of Rae Lee. I have new callouses to prove it. Being a gentleman aggravates my dick. However, I understand no means no. "You didn't answer my original question, though."

"Which one, detective? You've asked quite a few." She takes a calming breath to hide her amusement, oozing confidence.

"I thought we agreed on Anson." I toss my shoulders back at her cheeky remark. "It was 'Do you date?'"

Rae Lee asked me. So it's fair game.

"People don't understand what it's like to be me. I got tired of explaining the unexplainable, pretending I was—I don't know, normal? Healthy? Not a complete head case? Softening my rough edges to make anyone else comfortable is irritating. So no, I don't date anymore."

Rae Lee's reasoning makes perfect sense. I've never appreciated when anyone I was dating pressed me for details on an active investigation. I had a retort ready in case Rae Lee was curious about which leads she provided panned out. Except she never asked, simply accepted there were certain aspects of my job I couldn't discuss. And her easy acceptance of that fact was a relief I haven't felt in ages.

I wasn't up to the task of a full-fledged relationship until I met Angeline. My partner got me. Before I knew it, Grant was all that remained of the woman I loved. So I pivoted, focusing my attention on him.

"What if someone asked you out who understood?"

"Are you that someone, Anson?" Her brow raises. "Or are you looking for an invitation to my bed tonight?"

Maybe it's neither. But uncertainty has me wondering if maybe it's both. What I do know is, "I want to see you again, Rae Lee." I dip my mouth, tentatively brushing my lips to hers. She doesn't hesitate kissing me back. I lean my forehead to hers and grip her neck, threading my fingers through her blonde hair. "I've held off on saying good night because walking away from you feels like I could be walking away from something important."

She reaches up. Her thumb caresses my five o'clock shadow. "Going upstairs might be a bad start to a relationship, and having sex with me now that you know who I am is unprofessional."

Rae Lee turns, unlocking her door. I step off of the porch, intending on telling her to sleep well. I direct my attention to the grass, attempting to compartmentalize any emotion. I have her number. If I want to pursue Rae Lee, I'm not against using the case updates as a reason to contact her.

"Anson?" One hand on the knob, she looks over her shoulder, calling my name. "Are you coming?"

Rae Lee doesn't have to ask me twice. I press my palm to her back ascending the stairs and walking down a short hallway.

"This is really you," I say as we enter her apartment.

It's small—about the size of my living room and kitchen—an eclectic mix of old meets new, similar to the woman herself. Pipe shelving spans the interior wall, holding everything from her hanging wardrobe and folded sweaters and jeans to plastic drawers of her jewelry-making supplies. In between she's placed framed snapshots, her laptop, a digital camera, and other weird things single guys don't decorate with because we haven't been taught to. One area nearest the door is set up as a backdrop, presumably to photograph items she sells online. Seeing her space is like cracking a case. All of the pieces come together. My initial underestimation of Rae Lee was foolish.

The only furniture she has is a large round table with two chairs, a uniquely painted dresser, and a queen-size bed. The covers are indented, making me think back to her comment about how she naps a lot.

"Shoes by the door." Rae Lee flicks off her

sandals, relieving me of any guilt I feel for keeping her awake.

I toe mine off. It's another thing about her that seems right, and Rae Lee isn't acting as if she wants me to leave.

Our fingers entwine. She leads me around the table, towards the bed. I take slow, measured steps.

"So you have your handcuffs with you, right?" she asks, working the side zipper on her skirt. The *whoosh* it makes dropping to her feet mirrors my breath leaving my lungs.

"What!" I'm caught off guard by the woman standing before me, barefoot in only a tee and panties.

"I'm kidding." She giggles, placing her hand on my chest. "This time." She winks.

I grab hold of her wrist. My jaw hangs lower than it should.

"If you're not into… I mean, you can… Go. If you want. I just. You… It was a joke. You seemed tense." Rae becomes as squeamish as I was outside. Her skirt covering the floor is suddenly interesting.

"I don't want to leave," I say, tipping her chin towards me. "I hadn't planned on this. I didn't bring protection and…" I wipe my face. There's no polite way of saying no matter if Rae is on birth control or not, we're using a condom. "I'm a stickler about it."

"I've got *it* covered." She lets go, padding to the dresser and plucking foil square from the top dresser drawer. She hands it to me between her index and middle finger.

"Rae Lee, I think you're perfect." I take it and toss it onto the bed.

She blushes. I take her face in my palms and sweep my tongue into her mouth. She reaches for the hem of my shirt, untucking it from the waistband of my pants. Our clothes shed and fall on the floor. Rae Lee scampers towards the headboard. She crooks her finger with a teasing smile, beckoning me to join her.

I clutch her ankle instead and drag her back to the edge. We aren't strangers to one another's bodies, but I haven't gotten the chance to see Rae Lee naked, and here she is laid before me. I intend to soak her in.

"Anson, please don't make me beg for your cock." Her left hands glides up, circling around her breast. Plucking a pert little nipple that's begging for attention.

Her knees fall apart and her pussy glistens, tempting me.

"I won't." I've wanted a taste of Rae for weeks. When I'm done eating her out, she won't have the ability to string together two words, let alone beg.

I take a knee, batting Rae Lee's wandering hand as her fingers attempt to massage her clit. It's mine. Mine to tease. Her body is finally my playground to play at as I please.

I brace my palms on the soft skin of her thighs, spreading her legs farther apart. I want to see all of her. My tongue slides into her hot, wet folds with a leisurely lick. A moan escapes Rae's lips. Her hips lift from the mattress and her finger curls around my ear as I lap her sweet juices.

I notch two fingertips, nudging her entrance but not pushing in. My thumb circles her clit. My tongue rasps a hairsbreadth from the swollen pink bundle of nerves, driving her mad with anticipation.

"Please, sto—p," she stutters, reaching one hand to her head. The other grasps the back of my neck. Her fingernails dig into my scalp, trying to push my face closer to her cunt to stop the torture.

I laugh. I want Rae on tenterhooks. I'm rewarded with her keening squeals when my fingers curl inside of her and her hips buck. My cock throbs, craving its chance. I wrap my hand around my dick, pumping slowly while Rae Lee chases each sensation as I suck and finger fuck her.

Rae Lee has a beautiful mouth. If I blow my load bringing her to the edge, I have no doubt rebounding won't take long. Hell, since we met, I've hardly fisted myself in the shower without getting hard a second time thinking about her lips wrapped around my length. It's gotten so bad, sometimes I need an immediate encore after toweling off.

Feeling her inner walls tightening, I stand and drag my cock through her wetness. I bend her knees to her chest and collapse on top of her, thrusting into her tight, slick channel and working her body higher until it vibrates.

Unable to catch her breath, Rae squeaks tiny syllables of incomplete words. *Yes. More. Please. God. Harder. Fuck me.* She gasps clawing at my back, seeking her release.

I have her where I want her. The rhythm of our hips matches thrust for thrust. When I can't hold off any longer—when her orgasm overtakes every molecule in her body and it grabs hold of me like a vice—my balls tighten and my vision blurs. I spill into her, envisioning taking her like this over and over.

Deep in my chest, I'm positive there's something about this woman I won't ever get enough of.

And then Rae says the single word I wanted to hear most tonight...

Again.

Chapter Ten

Anson

Rae Lee plays with my St Rita medal, pressing it to my lips. "Kiss it for good luck."

The sun has just risen. Light filters through the seams between the windowsills and the shades. We're lying on our sides, talking quietly and lounging in her bed.

My lips push against the medal until she drops it, and then I kiss Rae Lee's nose. I haven't told her that I need all the luck I can get today. It feels like she already knows.

"I have to go soon." I run a finger over the swell of her breast.

I don't promise to call. I will. Or say that we'll see one another again later this week. That'll happen too. Except we've invested a lot of energy into finding Pearl Tatton and work has to come first.

Rae Lee nods, pressing her lips to my stubbled chin.

Eventually, I'll make a dumb guy move. We'll exchange words. Maybe she'll forgive me for whatever it is that I do. Maybe she won't. Maybe I'll be a pigheaded bastard and Rae Lee will dig her heels in and whatever we're starting will fall the fuck apart.

But right now, Rae Lee innately understands that what I need most is her patience.

I wish I could tell her how important today is to the case. Instead, I tuck a wayward lock of blonde hair behind her ear and tell her how beautiful she is. I'm graced with a soft thank you and a blush.

It was the blush I'd been going for. I found out that Rae Lee's light complexion makes her skin heat and she pinkens all over. Every possible way to make her blush is something I plan to thoroughly investigate next time we're together. Preferably naked.

I get out of bed in search of my clothes. Rae Lee gets up too, boiling water and pouring us steamy cups of tea. I bob the tea infuser in and out of my cup, making the water darker and sip, grateful it's not decaf. I'll pick up an Americano and a cinnamon bun—scratch that, I want two chocolate croissants—at Baked Beans in transit to the park.

This morning has the propensity to go south for someone. Even if a fraction of the pieces come together, it'll be a long one, that's for sure.

Dressed, I slip my phone in my pocket and pat myself down for my keys. "I swear for the amount of tedious things I lose, it has gotta be paranormal," I joke.

"No. She doesn't move anything," Rae Lee says

with a straight face over her porcelain teacup.

"Who?" I can't tell if she's joking.

"No one." Her eyes dart away as if her wall of craft supplies owns her interest, though she's been gawking at my ass while I got dressed.

No offense taken. I'd watched her slip a silk robe over her body. My fingers are itching to take it off of her before she showers.

"Is there a…" Ghost? At my place? Following me around?

"I didn't say that," she balks.

She didn't *not* say that either. I sit on the edge of the bed with my shoulders slumped. "Tell me the truth."

"You were there when she died. She's given me the impression you're unhappy and it makes her sad."

Angeline. Her divorce was finalized. She and Grant had moved in with Angeline's mother. She'd finally trusted me with everything that had gone wrong in her marriage. All of the mistakes she felt like she'd made. All of the domestic abuse cases she investigated, giving advice to the survivors that made her feel like a hypocrite. She feared something as simple as seeing a business card would set her ex-husband off, and she memorized the hotline numbers in case one day she needed to call.

The closer we got, the more she shared how guilty she felt pretending she wasn't a victim. And the remorse she had the day things went past the point of no return and Grant's father intentionally struck their child to make her bend to his will.

We stopped hiding that our friendship changed into a relationship. We were going to see where things led. She'd found stability. I was ready, willing, and able to step up and be the one to leave Brighton P.D. so that Angeline didn't find herself having to start over again, this time in her career.

"He shot her. Point blank. In the street." I shake my head, reliving the unfairness of it all in slow motion.

Along with several units, we'd responded to an emergency. Unbeknownst to anyone, Angeline's ex had tailed us. She got out of the car and so did he. Then he took aim three times, focusing on where ballistic vests don't cover, intending to do the most damage. Tale as old as time, it didn't matter what the courts said, her abuser had no intention of letting go. I can still feel Angeline's blood pouring through my fingers as I tried to put pressure on her neck wound.

"It wasn't your fault." Rae Lee touches my arm.

My vision blurs. I blink the misty eye away. "What Angeline went through wasn't hers either. She didn't deserve to die… Neither did Pearl."

I'm a good man. A good cop. But the thoughts about what I'd do to the guy *if only* creep in. Adrenaline amps me up. It makes my skull pound.

I rest my head in my hands. Rae Lee's body encircles mine. Talking about how amazing Angeline was is one thing. However, discussing her death slices at old wounds. Rae Lee holds me, whispering things I've wondered about. Repeating advice and words of forgiveness I've given to others that I've needed to heed myself. I haven't felt connected to anyone since Angeline. Not that I've gone out of my way to do anything about that. Perhaps that's what Angeline is trying to do for me; making me get my head out of my ass. I don't know any reason why Rae Lee and I would've crossed paths otherwise.

I turn and catch Rae Lee's lips. "Thank you for giving me closure."

Grief is funny. It sneaks around the corner when you least expect it. Though, I have a sense of peace I haven't felt in quite a while. Relief from the angst and ambiguity surrounding her daughter's disappearance is exactly the feeling I intend to get for Pearl Tatton's mother.

A short while later, Rae Lee walks me down the stairs. I skim my fingers over the sleeves of her soft robe and we say goodbye. I get home with enough time to shower and don fresh clothes and am fortunate enough that the line at Baked Beans moves fast.

Pulling into the park's parking lot, I pass Chaim. He's talking to the Parks and Rec Administrator. They're standing outside of an eight-foot fence draped with a standard blue canvas tarp for privacy that surrounds the well and extends out to include several feet of the walkway into the park.

When I reach them to say hello, Chaim's got his

hands in his pockets, completely nonchalant. Friendly when shaking my hand, the administrator's return to a folded position across his chest. Considering that the crew has to dig slowly—and that we haven't been upfront with him about what evidence we used to petition the court for the search warrant—I don't blame the guy for wanting to be here.

It feels like a cliché to stand around drinking coffee and eating pastry while waiting for the backhoe operator to start the engine. But cops have got to eat sometime. If any evidence turns up, Chaim and I have no idea when our next meal might be.

"Tried that new beer at Mark-39," I say around a mouthful of sweet.

Chaim swallows a swig of coffee. "Figures. I'll take the wife this week."

"Rain check, remember. Choose a night and dinner's on me." I'll ask Rae Lee to come too.

The rest of the town maintenance crew arrives. They start with jackhammers, efficiently demolishing the well. Chunks of debris fall, clattering and breaking into smaller pieces.

It's loud without ear coverings. I'm glad for the noise. The morning runners were having trouble getting past the fence. The decibel level along with the trucks and dumpster parked along the road will keep people away.

"Want to look at any of the debris before we move it?" The park administrator asks over the whiny *beep-beep-beep*.

The crew prepares to use a small loader to move the rubble into the dumpster.

"Anything unusual?" I squint, leaning in. Based on how the maintenance crew is treating our mere presence, they would've alerted Chaim or me if they uncovered something strange. We're more concerned about what's under the surface than above, anyhow.

"Negative. Is that good news or bad?"

"Depends who's asking." Chaim chuckles, receiving a weak smile from the administrator.

The detritus removed, the park crew gets back to work. They pull up the sidewalk where they began the day's work. It's the opposite of where I want them to dig. The morning passes agonizingly slow. The sun is high in the sky and the humidity is creeping up. The tree canopy provides decent shelter. It's as if we've had nothing better to do than scroll our phones for hours. Chaim is as bored as I am and takes our trash to a bin. My cell dings with an incoming email as he moseys back into the walled areas. I pocket it instead of reading.

"What took you so long?" He's gone as long as the longest construction crew member's break was.

"Restroom by the parking lot." His grunt is as good an offer as any for me to take a break.

I get back as the cement cracks in half on the first of two square pavers we're interested in. The ones whose sides Morris painted fluorescent orange that make the vee. The second one crumbles, and the crew moves the chunks. And then they stand there looking between the compact sand and Chaim and me.

"Christ." I roll up my sleeves and grab a shovel.

"How far down are you digging?" one crew member asks.

"Not a clue." I grit my teeth, stabbing the tip into the ground.

"We can pull up a layer at a time. A few inches?"

"That'd be great." I throw the shovel to the side, frustrated when I shouldn't be.

It doesn't change my mind about wanting to date Rae Lee, but this could be where things go awry. When she finds out we followed her leads, it can't be to a dead end. The problem is it's not even about my pride. Or perhaps it is. Is it selfish to want to uncover proof of Rae Lee's gift so I can tell her how proud I am of her?

Except, I also want it for Susan Turner, who's waited over a decade for answers. And most of all I want it for Pearl.

The loader skims a fraction of the sand away. I snap on gloves and rummage through the bucket. It's mostly gnarls with an occasional stick. Morris mentioned the ground shifts when it rains, so I chalk it up to that. Chaim inspects the remaining ground. And we start over until hitting a layer of dirt. That's when we notice it's mixed with the sand and uneven. It resembles a rock outcrop on the highway that has fallen over on its side.

The crew stays on the grass watching us. I use the shovel to loosen what I can. Sure enough, the largest bump has an unusual u-shaped indent and bulge where the vee was. Chaim and I agree to have additional layers skimmed. We sift through that too. Nothing. All this effort is proving pointless.

We're standing in the hole deciding what comes next. The administrator tells us that the city wouldn't have excavated for a sidewalk any lower that what's been dug.

I rub my tight neck, attempting to loosen the tension in my shoulders. I happen to look down as the park administrator shifts his weight. I see something move under his shoe.

"Move! Move!" I yell, crouching down to lift up a blue plastic corner.

Another tarp.

It yields a worn grommet and woven side, roughened by the elements. Before processing what I'm doing, I claw at the dirt. Dirt and wrinkled, weathered tarp lift away.

And then I stop.

"What do you have?" Chaim's shadow falls over me.

"Partial skull. And molars." Lower mandible is my best guess based on years of training. "I think we found her."

Chapter Eleven

Rae Lee

"Hey!" I chirp happily after pressing the speakerphone button to answer Anson's call. "I didn't expect to hear from you today."

Forensic analysis concluded the remains found in the park were Pearl's. I attended the funeral at Susan Turner's behest. She's messaged me several times since, wanting to contact Pearl. As Anson is still working the case, I've put her off. She's certain if we connect I'll provide additional leads.

It's been a hard-won argument. But I say no because I learned the hard way I have to consider my health. Right now putting me first includes spending as much time as humanly possible with a certain Brighton Police detective.

"I wasn't going to call, but—" The sound on Anson's side of the line gets muffled. "Listen, I'm outside. Can I come up?"

"Sure. The back door's open." I hear him growl. I understand the guy who has escorted me to the rear entrance after every single date we've had is concerned for my safety, but... "Nobody's getting in who shouldn't, grumpy pants. Layla and Julian are in the yard trying to fix a lawn mower."

"I can't stay long. I have to swing by the Turners'." I hear a car door slam.

"Fine by me." I knew as much.

Anson huffs, approaching the house. "Hanging up now."

I've gotten used to the modicum of efficiency Anson uses communicating. Due to the odd hours he finds himself on-duty, his schedule winds up all over the place. Coincidentally, that peculiarity fits perfectly with the wild swings my sleep schedule often takes.

The nicest part is Anson is considerate when I'm having a rough day. He's as happy to grab takeout on his way over, and nap next to me after we've gorged ourselves on them, as I am to create at three in the morning while he's in dreamland, making up for lost sleep.

For our first double date, Anson and I met Chaim and his wife for beers at Mark-39. We shared trays of loaded fries and talked for hours. With Julian's help, we scored pre-sale tickets to an amazing show at Sweet Caroline's next week. I'm so excited for the performance. Julian's even taking the night off so Layla has someone to dance with.

Last night, Paisley's Boutique had an open house. I'd thought the engraved invitation I received was because the shop stocks my jewelry. Nope! Layla wanted to introduce me to her friends. They were so nice—and when Layla encouraged me to share how Anson and I wound up together, *not one of them* asked me to channel their long-lost relative. Meanwhile, Anson went to watch Grant's baseball game and stayed at Angeline's mother's for dinner.

Which is to say, so far so good! We're not rushing things and have made the best of the time we've had together so far.

I also kinda like it that Anson pretends my earbuds are in when we're in public and I murmur, "Sorry, can't talk now." I feel... a little less like people think I'm the weird girl.

The knob to my apartment jiggles moments later. He kicks the door with his toe, holding a liquor box from the ABC store with two hands.

"Whatcha got there?" I ask. It's too early to drink, but curiosity has the best of me.

Anson blows out a deep breath. "A present. Maybe. If you want to keep it."

My mouth forms an "o". I didn't realize that there was an appropriate anniversary gift for dating

—

I stop and use my fingers to tick off the weeks, giving up after what counted as Anson's third weekend off. We've done enough together that it doesn't seem to matter how long we've been seeing one another. Well, that and I'm over the moon that there's a hot cop here with a present for me.

Can life get any better than that? I don't think so.

I slide my supplies to the side, and he slides the box on the table. I stand up to peer into the box, but Anson beats me to it, reaching in.

My fingertips fly to my mouth when the box makes a tiny meow.

"Grant and I found this poor slob in the crawl space under his grandmother's house." My boyfriend holds up an itty-bitty orange kitten with big blue eyes. It cries out, opening its tiny mouth and stretching its limbs.

"For me?" I gently take him from Anson, snuggle his little body over my breasts, and rub my chin against his soft fur.

Anson's lips tip up. He pets the cat and curls his palm behind my ear, moving the hair that's fallen forward.

"If you want him. If not, I'll drop him off at the shelter. I've already made a vet appointment. The receptionist asked his name. I said I'd get back to them about it. 'Cat' seemed unimaginative."

My heart swells that Anson intends to take care of him and not leave the responsibility of caring for a cat that hasn't had its shots to the overburdened shelter. But my tummy also bumps over the hump of a roller coaster and bottoms out. I don't want this defenseless animal left alone.

"What about Grant? Won't his grandmother let him keep the kitten?"

"Grant kept *his* sister." He scratches the tabby boy kitten's head and back. "She's black and white and, boy, can she vocalize. Grant named her Harper."

"Then we give Fred a good home."

"Fred?"

"Yes, because he bears a striking resemblance to Paul... Don't you. Don't you." I baby-talk, holding Fred up to my nose and wiggle.

"I don't understand."

"I don't expect you would. Chalk it up as another one of life's great mysteries." I peck Anson on the lips and thank him for the kitten. "Fred makes my heart happy. You make my heart happy," I say. It's too soon for I love you, but that's what I mean.

"You make my heart happy, too, Rae Lee."

My heart skips a beat and my lips part, startled at his words. Anson's unabashed grin tells me we're on the same page about where this relationship is headed.

He leans in to kiss me goodbye and his velvety tongue swipes against mine. I wrap an arm around his neck, cautious not to crush the ball of fur cradled between us. He pulls my lower body flush to his and his arousal presses at my belly. My inner thighs warm.

Anson picks up on my legs shifting. I wiggle, trying to satisfy the ache until we're in bed together again.

"You have a problem there, Rae?"

"Not one I can't solve on my own." I wink.

His eyes shift toward my dresser, then back to mine. A woman doesn't have to be clairvoyant to know what Anson is thinking. I was a single gal for a while. There are more items in the top drawer than lingerie and a new box of condoms.

"Don't." Kiss. "You." Kiss. "Dare."

Anson

The single most part of this job I despise is being responsible for informing a family that they've lost a loved one. Though Brighton P.D.'s crime scene investigation unit trucks parked away from prying eyes, a reporter got wind of our presence at the park. So when Chaim brought in the county coroner's office to assess our findings, and the local news immediately picked up the story and ran with it for the four o'clock news, I felt the ticking time bomb of impending doom.

Despite my hunch being correct and being proud of Rae Lee's because the new leads she provided panned out, there's no glory in solving this case. A little girl still died. A mother still grieves.

Using dental records and DNA, the state's forensic pathologist identified the teeth and skull as belonging to Pearl Tatton. It was a fluke we had any remains at all. Though her assailant wrapped her small body in a tarp, time was unkind and nature ran its course. A few years from now, there'd hardly be a shred of evidence left. The things Pearl showed Rae Lee wouldn't tie together with what I saw with my own two eyes. The hard proof I need to go on as a cop would be non-existent. As would the confidence I have in my girlfriend's experiences with the afterlife.

In retrospect, Mrs. Turner's insistence that we bring Rae Lee in on the case wasn't a great deal of comfort to her the day I sat Susan down to share the news that we finally found her daughter. I was glad the department had something to return to her at all. However, seeing her child, holding Pearl's whole healthy and living body is something I regret not being able to do. As was Susan's ability to have an open casket at Pearl's memorial, which Rae Lee and I attended.

I was hardly out of the police academy at the time of Pearl's disappearance. Yet—akin to the days after Angeline's fatal shooting—the feeling like I hadn't done enough persists. Not knowing what prompted Pearl to open the door the evening she disappeared haunts me. I hope the answers come soon.

Driving across town, the closer I get to the Turners' the more obvious it is that I need to get my wits about me. Although the maudlin thoughts have crept in, I'm happy to have left Rae Lee's on a positive note. Grant was worried about separating the cats, but when he chose the black one my gut trusted the other belonged with Rae Lee.

By naming the kitten Fred, Rae Lee dangled a mystery in front of me. It's a puzzle I intend to solve. Saint Rita hasn't led me astray so far.

Susan greets me at the door. She looks happy to see me. My insides churn. The latest update is sure to break apart whatever pieces of her heart she's mended.

"Do you recognize this man, Susan?" I show her a printout with two pictures of the suspect we've identified. Side-by-side, the first image was taken over a decade ago.

Susan's eyes track to the recent photo. The man's hair is grayed. His cheeks gaunt. The drab jumpsuit he's wearing adds years to his age. She's about to give a clipped nod and say no, when she shifts her gaze and focuses on the suspect as a younger man.

"Alan." Susan's face pinches. Tears fill her eyes and her chin wobbles.

It's evident when it clicks for Pearl's mother the way it had for me.

What Susan and I heard the day of Rae Lee's walk-through was Pearl left on a dare. That was even Rae Lee's initial interpretation.

But Pearl was emphatic and Rae Lee repeated over and over *It was a dare.*

The email I hadn't opened during the excavation at the park was the Town of Brighton Parks and Recreation entire employment records going back to the department's inception.

At the top of the list was a short-term hire.

Alan *Adair.*

A name so clearly visible that I hadn't noticed it at first glance.

Shocked, Susan turns to Harvey. Her lip trembles as she regards her husband. "Pearl. She was unhappy we were seeing each other after her father died. I broke things off and dated Alan. But it was impossible not to see Harvey at work. So I called it off with Alan," she explains for my benefit.

"How long were you involved with Mr. Adair?"

She places the paper on the coffee table. "A few months."

"Was it serious?"

"No. Not on my part. Between the business and Harvey helping out around the house, I'd been torn."

"What was Adair's reaction to you deciding not to date him any longer?"

Susan's shoulder's hit her ears. "Alan was upset. He said he wasted a lot of time trying to make things work with me."

"Do you think he was resentful?"

"I—I don't know. He told me he was leaving town after I broke it off. I didn't see him afterwards."

"You have a timeframe between the last time you

spoke with Alan Adair and the evening Pearl went missing?"

"I'd been back with Harvey for four weeks. Maybe more? I haven't even thought of Alan since," Susan says, bewildered. As if she should have thought harder, racked her overwhelmed brain at a time when the primary emotion a parent feels is sheer terror.

"What was Adair's relationship with Pearl like?"

"Good. He went out of his way to include her when…"

"When?" I prompt after Susan's pregnant pause.

"When I told Alan that Pearl seemed resentful of Harvey taking her father's place. Oh God, did I?" Susan takes a choking gasp. "Pearl went with Alan didn't she? Was it my fault?"

I lean in, taking Susan's hands in mine. "The person responsible was the one who took your child. Remember that. Always."

"Where is he? Where is Alan now?" Pearl's mother sounds panicked.

"Alan Adair has been incarcerated in Texas. He was found guilty of trying to murder his second wife after a kidnapping."

If Susan Turner needs the rest of the story, she can search it out. It's ugly. Adair intended to ransom the baby he'd stolen.

Along with a victim statement calling to light the safety of another child in the same family, Brighton P.D.'s quiet interest in Adair recently swayed the parole board from releasing him.

And while his lawyer argues that it's neither here nor there, since Adair knew Susan Tatton, the penitentiary's search of his personal effects has found articles pertaining to the Pruitt murders and Pearl Tatton's disappearance. The lawyer also takes exception to the partial fingerprints found at the scene. Years ago, investigators hadn't been able to match those prints because Adair's weren't entered into the system until he was booked for his arrest.

We're slowly building a case that Adair—a grifter—ingratiated himself to Pearl. That he came to the Tattons' that night in an attempt to reconcile with Susan, who had inherited a sizable amount upon her husband's death. And that sometime after Pearl opened the door, Adair hit her on the head with her softball bat. Trace metal fragments were embedded in the bone. He cleaned the bat with the hand towel and hid it under Pearl's bed. Then the park maintenance worker brought her body, wrapped in the tarp, to the park and buried her next to the wishing well where he knew the town was putting the sidewalk because he was on the crew.

Except the following day, Adair failed to show up for work. He'd moved to Texas and moved on to bilk another unsuspecting widow.

Rae Lee

"Can I ask you something?" Susan rolls her lips.

I have a duty to see this through, but couldn't agree to meet Pearl's mother before the prosecutor presented his case against Alan Adair. I knew whatever came out during the trial would create new uncertainties for Susan. Except, I also have to protect myself and the life Anson and I are building together. Because of that, I can only speak to Pearl again this once to help her mom heal.

We have a blanket spread at Pearl's gravesite. Susan brought a basket filled with petit fours and teacups she allowed Pearl to play tea party with before Pearl's father died. It's an unusual place for a picnic … nowadays. A long time ago, people used to spend time with their dead relatives this way. Some cultures still do.

"Of course." I'm here to finally answer any lingering questions Susan has.

"Did Pearl ever say, show you, tell you why she had a problem with Harvey?"

Unspeaking, I place my hand over hers. Our eyes lock. My nod is weak. I don't want to hurt Susan any more than she has been.

Anson shielded me from most of the press coverage, but, to make up for his initial reaction to me, my boyfriend needs to prove to me that he believes there are truths to what the dead tell me. So when Adair tried to plead by throwing Harvey Turner under the bus, we'd had a very long, in-depth discussion about my original concerns that Pearl was molested.

"I—I thought so." Susan frowns. The Turner's marriage hadn't survived Adair's accusations. "Pearl's best friend came to me after the funeral. I didn't want to believe Ellen at first. I didn't want to be the love fool who dismissed her daughter's worries. But I'd already wondered for years about the face cloth found in the bathroom hamper. To the point that I can't quite recall the details of the day clearly." She huffs a sad sigh. "It was a horribly long day."

"I'm sure it was," I agree.

My interactions with Pearl are different outside of their home. She danced around the blanket and sat next to her mother, leaning in and squeezing her arm. She's angelic. Younger today. About the age that she might've enjoyed an afternoon tea party.

During this visit, Pearl showed me how everything had gotten so complicated for Susan when her first husband fell ill. She'd been managing her home, caring for a sick spouse and trying to keep their business afloat in a bad economy.

I've felt the emptiness in Pearl's chest the moment she feels like she's awoken from the blow to her head. It mirrors the loneliness and heartache emanating from Susan both then and now. Pearl has always struggled with her mother not having any more children. They couldn't be Harvey's. But now Pearl is aware her mother has no one to rely on outside of the grief recovery and support group she's attending. I encourage Susan to spend an afternoon with Ellen. It's never too late to mend bridges. Ellen is healing, too.

Our picnic is over a little while later when Anson's car pulls into the cemetery to bring me home.

We tidy from the picnic and stride across the grass arm in arm. Along the way, I nod and mouth my appreciation to the unseen others who wanted my attention, but respected it was Pearl and Susan's turn for closure.

"Thank you, Rae Lee, for finding my daughter." Susan hugs me when we get to where the cars are parked.

"You're welcome," I say, returning her embrace. "I have something for you." I pop a box out of my bag and press it into her palms. "Open it when you get home."

Inside is a pearl I hand wrapped with silver and fashioned into a pendant. My jewelry business is doing well. Anson and I use the L word. He, Fred, and I are so happy we're moving in together soon.

I have a life to lead, but I want Pearl's mother to know neither of them will ever be far from my thoughts.

Thank you for reading Fragments of the Past! I hope you enjoyed puzzling the pieces together with Rae Lee and Anson as much as I loved it when *they showed me* who was guilty of the crime!

What will an obsessive alpha like Jake Ballentine, the owner of Sweet Caroline's, risk to stay in control? Enjoy the following preview of **Bleeding Heart**, a runaway bride, enemies to lovers romance!

BLEEDING HEART

Paisley

"Paisley, will you have Gavin as your lawfully wedded husband, to live together in the covenant of matrimony? Will you love him, comfort him, honor and keep him, in sickness and in health, and forsaking all others, keep you only unto him, for the rest of your life?"

The end of the minister's sentence fades,

overcome by the loud whooshing in my ears. Sweat that has already dampened the satin at my armpits and down the back of my gown, making the soft fabric itchy and uncomfortable, now trickles between my breasts. My breaths come in short pants. My heart, searching for escape, is threatening to beat outside of my chest. Not literally, though once a man like Gavin held it cradled in their hands as gently as my husband-to-be is holding my hands.

My tongue darts to wet my parched lip. The underside gets caught on the smudge-proof lipstick the makeup artist applied. We've spared no expense for this wedding. I'd seen candelabras. Gavin suggested the ceremony be at night. And the chapel is lit by candlelight! We are what everyone deems perfect for one another.

Gavin loves me. I love him. How could I not? He's a good man.

But do I not honor Gavin and devalue our relationship by continuing with this wedding? Or do I love him enough to be the "anyone who knows a reason" why we shouldn't marry one another?

keep you only unto him
for the rest of your life

I'd abide by those words if somewhere deep in my gut my shriveling soul was interpreting them the same way that Gavin is.

That's what I have.

A black soul for playing along with a lie until it

was too late and embarrassing Gavin in public.

We're in a church, for Christ's sake!

Oh, crap. If I weren't spinning the wheel trying to decide which path to hell the arrow will point me in, then taking Lord's name in vain has added a short, direct route.

Lightheaded, I wrap my left hand over my stomach and bend at the waist. Gavin's thumb presses into the top of my left hand. His fingers pinch into my palm.

"Paisley, are you okay?" His voice filled with concern, Gavin shifts his stance so that he's shielding me from the pews occupied by our family and Gavin's friends and colleagues from the hospital.

"Just, *ah*, give me a sec." The sheer fabric of my veil flops over my shoulder, covering my watery eyes. I try some deep breathing exercises. My chest aches. My fingertips are cold and tingling. Perspiration drenches my scalp.

My mother's compliment from before she escorted me down the aisle rushes at me like a tidal wave. *You're going to have the most beautiful marriage, Paisley. I'm so happy you found a man that loves you unconditionally and that you have a bright beginning, similar to what your father and I had.*

I wanted to tell my mom that Gavin's love comes with strings attached. That he couldn't keep me only unto him, no matter how short our life together winds up being. Gavin needs more.

I can't live trapped in the cage of domestic bliss.

I don't want him to kiss me goodbye in the morning and drive away in his BMW, pretending I'm the woman he still wants.

Both of us can't lie.

I can't marry Gavin.

And now that I've made up my mind, I'm in a huge pickle, aren't I?

"Oh, gosh!" I whip my head back, standing ramrod straight. I brush away the layers of tulle resting on my head to get them out of my face. When that doesn't work, I grip the tiny pearl and silver tiara from Sterlings that the veil is attached to and rip it entirely out of my hair. Giving Gavin a wide-eyed and wily smile, I'm positive he's ready to have me committed to the psychiatric wing.

"Sweetheart?" Gavin's gaze is wrought with concern.

"You are going to make an amazing husband." I pat underneath the knot in his silk cravat. "But you shouldn't waste the happiness the world has to offer you on me."

I turn toward the chancel and bolt. My skirt swishes past the altar and I duck out the door in front of the minister's vestry. The corridor leads to the stairs, to the lower floor where I waited to march down the aisle, and outside to the parking lot.

"Paisley!" Gavin yells.

I doubt he'll stay put. I mean, would any groom if they were questioning why their bride left them at the altar? But I don't have an answer Gavin will accept. He'll coerce me back inside and I'll give in so as not to disappoint anyone.

The streetlights above light up the sky the moment I step outside. It casts a glow over the rows of parked cars, highlighting that none are of any use without a set of keys. The limo driver, charged with whisking the new Dr. and Mrs. Gavin Laughton to the reception, is waiting at the entrance of the church. Quickly, I realize I've skipped from one problem to the next. I need to find my way out of here.

"This is why robbers don't wait until the last minute to figure out their getaway plan, Paisley!" I chastise myself aloud.

I lift my gown off the blacktop, ball it in my fists, and start running. My high heels pinch my toes when my feet land on the pavement, making my lips twist. *Shoot!* I was sorely mistaken thinking the blisters I'd have by the end of tonight would be from dancing the night away.

I stop, hop up and down, remove my shoes, and let them clop to the ground. A twinge of guilt hits me. They were such nice shoes. It's followed by a second pang of regret. How can I be sad about ditching Jimmy Choos when I just left the man I was supposed to marry in the most compromising position anyone could find themselves in?

Well, maybe it's not *the* most. But getting ditched ranks up there for embarrassment. Poor Gavin. And my poor mother... *Eeeh.* My mother. I'll find a way to live this fiasco down, but can they?

"Paisley? Where are you?"

"Oh shit, he's still after me!" I squeak.

Skittering onto the cold and damp sidewalk, I pick up the pace. Within the next few blocks, I'm going to go from Historic Brighton to Downtown Brighton to the back alleyways that investment firms thought twice about revitalizing.

Beyond a chain link fence, flashing pink letters on a neon sign catch my attention. Almost out of breath from the heavy layers I'm carrying, I have two choices. I can keep running and risk the possibility of getting hepatitis when I step on a needle. Or I can duck inside and pray that Sweet Caroline's is the last place on earth anyone—especially a well-respected heart surgeon—will come looking for me.

There's a single car in the lot, so I take my chances that the customers won't think I'm part of the stage show. I scoot under an awning, ignoring the marquee advertising the scantily clad headline acts, and pull on a door handle.

"No, no. Don't be locked. Don't be locked!" I dare to glance over my shoulder, reaching for the other door.

Not as heavy as I expect, it swings open, nearly toppling me over. I step into the dark strip club, pulling my dress inside before I can't see anything anymore, and risk it catching between the doors. My practically bare feet can feel the holes in my stockings and the short pile of the rug.

"We're closed," booms a voice from down a dark

hall.

"I need to use the phone. Make a call." I arch my spine six ways from Sunday, trying to see in the shadows.

I'm also wondering who exactly am I calling? And how am I paying for the lift because my purse, with my phone and my credit cards, are in the church's undercroft.

Thank fuck I own a boutique because not making off with the money would make bank robbery an exceptionally poor career choice.

A tall silhouette emerges, back lit by the hallway. He uses the top of a liquor bottle to flip a switch, washing the entire theater in harsh light. I cover my eyes for them to adjust.

"Don't you have a cell?" The man demands, accusing me of being an idiot.

A whole congregation agrees you're not far off, dude.

"I lost it." Along with my sanity.

I blink, and the man across the room is staring at me in shock.

Can't say I blame him. I'm sort of shocked about how my night is going, too. Although, I'm the slightest bit more prepared for this encounter than Sweet Caroline's proprietor is.

From the looks of the desolate parking lot, I thought there would be a bartender in here. A bouncer. A regular watching a dancer spin around a pole, too enamored by the woman taking her clothes off on stage to become involved in my little circus act. After humiliating myself in front of two hundred people who I know, what difference would half a dozen who I don't make?

However, I hadn't factored Jake Ballentine into the mix.

No downtown business owner has to have met him to know him. Jake is a man whose reputation precedes him. His omnipotent presence in this small town is as much an institution as the gentleman's club he owns.

More than Jake's questionable dealings tower above. From across the room, he looms gigantic. Long and lean, Jake is dressed in crisp black trousers. His unbuckled belt jangles at his hips. Several buttons on his shirt are undone at the collar. The power in his neck and broad shoulders is similar to a competitive swimmer. His tie hangs loose. His blond hair is disheveled like he's gripped it at the root, but it appears he's also tried to mat it down and back into place.

I'm uncertain if the attempt to make himself look presentable is for my benefit. I would have buckled the belt first, but that's just me, and I'm a girl.

Jake strides over the carpeting with the bottle of amber liquid in his grip. He sets it on a small round table as he passes.

"I thought the princess lost a shoe leaving the ball?"

I crane my neck to reply. "Oh, I did that bitch one better." I lift the tattered hem of my soiled gown and wiggle my toes.

His cantankerous laughter bounces off the walls. "Come on, which one of the guys set me up?" He shakes his head, unbelieving. "I could have sworn Trig and Carver were having too much fun with their respective wives to notice I left."

I shake my head in response. "No clue what you are talking about. Didn't know you were closed. Didn't remember my cell."

Jake plays with the cleft in his square chin. His pupils are wide and black with an icy blue halo. He stares, daring me to hide the truth from him. "It can't be that simple."

"Uh, yeah. It can," I say sarcastically. It is the truth and I'm coming down from the adrenaline high of hot-footing it out of a church during my wedding. "So can I—"

The door flings open interrupting me.

"I need to use your phone. Please! I left mine at the church a few blocks away and I need to tell my fiancée's mother... Paisley?"

Oh, fuckkity, fuck, fuck.

My shoulders hit my ears. I'm caught in Jake's blue-eyed tractor beam, unable to turn and look at Gavin.

"Just go with it," I whisper under my breath.

I jump before even realizing what I'm doing. Wrapping my arms around his neck, the Norse God's palms encase my ass, and our bodies press flush together. Jake plays along, kissing me as if runaway brides barrel into his establishment every single day, searching for sanctuary.

And while this kiss isn't the one I anticipated ending my wedding day with, I have to admit Jake Ballentine is an amazing kisser.

Ready to read more?
Bleeding Heart is available now!
www.jodykaye.com/bleedingheart

Add your voice and help readers discover this love story by writing a review!

Author Notes

About three hundred and seventy million books ago… Okay, it's more like fifteen other sixteen, but it feels like much more… I dedicated a book to a long-time friend, who I am happy to say is still a part of my life. In the author notes section, I mentioned someday I'd write something amazing, edgy, and most importantly, paranormal for them—when I figured out how.

So, Sarah, I know there are no chapters with vampires wearing combat boots, but I *think* this the book. And I hope you love it.

I have to give credit where it is due, though. Laramie Briscoe approached me, asking if I'd consider writing a romance true-crime style. I desperately needed an idea that energized me. However, what I knew then about grizzly topics was this: if anything creeped me out on TV, I was turning the channel. That goodness I'm a reader. LOL.

Laramie, you've always been a go-to person for author support. Thank you for the times you've taken me under your wing and thank you for having faith that I could fly with this short story.

To AK MacBride, Heidi McLaughlin, Samantha Bacca, Lucinda Race, and Kate Farlow. Thanks for the boost when author self-doubt crept in.

To all of my amazing readers who enthusiastically got behind me trying something new, especially Kim and Meg: I write the final version of every story with you in mind. I'm so honored to still have a place on your bookshelves.

Jill, you are important. Don't ever forget it.

MJA, your encouragement to write someone like Rae Lee reminds me how lucky I am to be the heroine in our love story. I love you more.

Also by Jody Kaye

————

Shattered Hearts of Carolina
Splinter of Hope
Shred of Decency
Sliver of Truth
Holding Onto Hope
Home Wrecker
Deep Gap
Bleeding Heart
Shattered Soul

Shattered Hearts of Carolina
Love Stories
Fragments of the Past

The Kingsbrier Legacy
Love Thy Neighbor
Gray Sin
Going Down
Love Me Fast
Rumor Has It
Measure of a Man
Never Get Over You

The Kingsbrier Quintuplets
Eric
Brier
Daveigh
Miss Cavanaugh
Cavanaugh
Adam
Colette
Colton

Kingsbrier Love Stories
All My Firsts: Tessa & Alcee

The Canvas Duet
Canvas
Imprint

About the Author

Jody's husband asked what she'd been doing all day. After five years she finally confessed, "When no one is around, I write."

Okay, it was more like a bunch of stammering and trying to get out of saying a thing. Jody's a writer. You want it pretty. Let's compromise.

"Just finish one," he said, challenging her to complete a story and share it. Little did he know that those words of encouragement meant they'd return from a family vacation with a wild and defiant set of quintuplets stumbling their way into adulthood. Wasn't raising their three sons enough?

A native of nowhere, Jody settled in New England for 17 years before agreeing to uproot her brood of boys and move to North Carolina. She's a part-time graphic designer and marketeer with over twenty years' experience, and full-time writer. If Jody ever gets lost, you'll find her reading, all the while hoping that her ravenous children haven't eaten all the ingredients before she's cooked dinner.

To view more great titles,
sign up for Jody Kaye's newsletter,
or find her on social media go to
www.jodykaye.com or

Scan Now!